THE LAST DAYS OF THE FIGHTING MACHINE

The Martians Are Dying

C. A. Powell

Copyright © 2019 C. A. Powell
All rights reserved.

Story Two: **The Martian Apocalypse of Victorian Britain.**

CONTENTS

Preface (Introduction) — vii

Chapter 1	The Crewmen of F.S. *Ney*	1
Chapter 2	The Constable of Canewdon	21
Chapter 3	Mad Dogs and Englishmen	43
Chapter 4	The Fighting Machine at Paglesham Churchend	67
Chapter 5	The Mud Banks of Wallasea Island	96
Chapter 6	The Horror in the Church	116
Chapter 7	Terror of the Woods	148
Chapter 8	Priming the Field Gun	166
Chapter 9	Attacking the Fighting Machine	203
Chapter 10	Back to the Field Gun	207
Chapter 11	Once More unto the Breach	243

Epilogue — 263

PREFACE (INTRODUCTION)

The War of the Worlds fell upon Victorian Britain in the summer of 1898. The destruction of civilization began in earnest as giant tripod fighting machines spread death and destruction on a scale unprecedented and unimagined.

The human race seemed doomed. But then the organised killing faltered. The Martian beings inside the fighting machines became ill to Earthly disease and pestilence. The organised formations broke down. The despicable giant monuments stood still in cities, towns and fields across the invaded lands. The few killing machines that still moved were more laboured. Many were solitary rogue units acting independently. The surviving Martians were desperate and less confident.

Human survivors crawled out from the destruction and desolation of the wretched landscape. And from these hidden places, some went on the offensive against the weakened Martian invaders.

CHAPTER 1

THE CREWMEN OF F.S. *NEY*

The night was gentle, with an eerily soft sea breeze. But merely eerie was pleasing: eerie was better than the Terror, much more acceptable than unbearable trepidation. Death had been the normal way of things. Extensive slaughter of the human race had been attempted. Many had witnessed diabolical events over recent months. Now the Terror was no longer apparent. It was just eerie, with the serene lapping of the sea against the ship's hull. Millions had died in a few weeks, but many had survived. The horrendous alien nuisance was no longer intense. Something had changed.

The international fleet had been cruising the English coastline for a number of days. There had been scattered sporadic incidents: ferocious offshore naval engagements with the huge Martian tripod fighting machines; a ship had been hit here and there; sometimes, a fighting machine fell under the intense barrage of fleet bombardment. But it was true – at first, it had just been rumours. Sailors commenting on how sluggish the alien machines looked. Yet thankfully it remained true. The ferocious intensity of the alien invasion had abated.

At first the Martian offensive had been a rampant and unmerciful attack lasting for many weeks. But then the power and concentration of the killings began to diminish. Queen Victoria's realm was in ruins, but the alien aggressors had lost direction. They seemed uncoordinated. Such all-powerful supremacy had rapidly diminished. Something was wrong with the invaders from space. But what, no one could say.

It was still difficult to enjoy the beautiful, clear night that was full of stars. Just the usual, normal, twinkling stars. The gorgeously common, clear night sky. No longer the ominous glowing wake of alien lights falling to Earth. Such things had been abundant a few weeks earlier. Now, everything had gone quiet from Mars. Just the odd scattered lumbering of a far-off fighting machine – distant gigantic vermin scurrying to hide from combined naval bombardments.

It would still be a long time before the tranquil havens could allow a feeling of charmed pleasure for the seamen of Queen Victoria's impotent, almost pointless, Royal Navy. She had been aided by fleets from France, Germany and other European countries. All the seamen, throughout the combined fleets, were of the same mind. The stars had lost their allure and naval power was of little use against land-based tripod fighting machines that were too far inland.

The combined fleets of many battleships steamed along the Essex coastline, northwards past Foulness Island. The area had become frighteningly unknown over the last few months. The forsaken County of Essex had been one of the regions overrun by the alien invaders.

Therefore, since the coming of the Martians and their hideous tripod fighting machines, the heavens had become a place of ominous and fantastic fear. The intensity and the multitude of aliens falling from the sky had destroyed what had once been wonder. These clear, sparkling stars aroused only dread. What other hideous monstrosities were out there and how insignificant were the men of Earth?

Upon the deck of one of the French Central battleships, F.S. *Ney*, an old and seasoned quartermaster, Pascal Blanc, leaned against the bulwarks and stared up at the heavens. A Heaven that allowed Hell to come to Earth. He muttered as much to himself, accusing the All-Knowing Unseen.

"Where are you now, God?"

He pursed his lips and his huge black moustache drooped above his bushy beard. With new contempt for the stars, he slowly shook his head in the night sea breeze. How long would it be before these Martians left the confines of Britain and began to spread out across the European continent? And then to the other great land masses of the Earth? Maybe that is why the aliens had gone quiet? Perhaps they were preparing for a second phase.

Suddenly, his contemplation was interrupted as a star shell shot out from one of the fleet's ships further forward along the convoy. The fizzing flare arched across the night sky, tearing across the estuary of the River Crouch towards land at Holliwell Point.

The coastline lit up over the distant shores, where the black silhouettes of two giant Martian tripods were abruptly exposed, bathed in the flare's radiance. The ghastly fighting machines stood like ominous sentinels waiting to engage the fleet as it steamed passed. The Martians' stealth was exposed. The ghastly abominations could not make good with their carefully prepared deceit.

Blanc's eyes widened in despair as he took stock of the sight. He cursed the two hideous monstrosities. All about him, men were running to action stations amid the sound of the ship's siren. More flares arced out over the coastline. The silhouettes of the alien fighting machines were now clear targets. The star shells allowed every vessel in the fleet an open field of fire. Gun turrets from a multitude of ships swung about. They opened fire at the shoreline, where the glowing machines were standing. At first, a sporadic and straddled affair. Then, more ship's guns began to open up; it quickly became a furious, ear-splitting roar of fire power, a diabolical firestorm of explosions, an inferno of biblical proportion. Along the line of battleships were bright flaming flashes of light as shell after shell spat out. A combined and enraged programme, one that the fleet had practised and tuned. Whenever the unearthly machines came to the coast, the ships of the international fleet could engage. And of late, the aliens had been sluggish. The Martian fighting machines' systems were slower.

Blanc crouched and put his hands to his ears as F.S. *Ney*'s guns lent her rage to the salvo of shells being hurled at Holliwell Point. The mighty battleship shuddered as each gun's detonation reverberated along the iron hull and wood-panelled deck. The man-made floating titans were impressive as explosions erupted all around the distant alien machines. Quartermaster Blanc raised his binoculars to his eyes and watched the gangling machines attempting to walk around the erupting earth and fire. One of the machines took a direct hit, and there was a cheer. He delighted in the sight of the flames and debris exploding upwards beneath the gruesome alien indignation, savouring the moment when one of its legs began to buckle. Then a feeling of elated joy when the Martian machine's orbed spy-window exploded in a ball of spewing flame. The colossal edifice seemed to screech in terror. Yet it was just a machine. The Martians within could not be heard at such a distance surely? An uncanny shriek ripped out across the night. Then the colossal edifice wobbled, two legs struggling to maintain balance. But it was to no avail. The burning contrivance fell forward into the exploding earth. A roar of approval rose as the titan vanished amid the dreadful upsurge of violent response. Gorgeous human fury. Wonderful and sublime.

Human hell!

The colossal machines were not invincible after all. They could fall before such combined might. The devastation was magnificent. The old quartermaster's adrenalin raced pleasurably through his veins. He savoured man's wild, uncontrolled anger; he felt wonder at his own callous and shallow brutality. The sight was beautiful, the slaughter was superb. Total blood lust. Blanc prized every moment of it.

It was to be a short-lived pleasure. With a high-pitched sound, the second machine retaliated. Its weapons screamed out. Javelins of cruel light ripped through the night air, rapid heat rays of spitting blue light. Ships within the convoy erupted as explosions tore through them. But the combined international fleets bravely blazed on, throwing everything each ship could muster at the remaining machine.

A young lieutenant had come up to the bulwarks next to Blanc, raised his binoculars to his eyes and whooped out in delight, as the second and more aggressive tripod took a hit. The excited young officer shouted to the old quartermaster:

"Another hit! That is the two of them." He yelled through the roar of the guns with youthful enthusiasm.

Blanc grinned at the young officer and replied with words of encouragement:

"Yes, sir. And I would wager more strikes very soon."

Then there was a blinding flash and an upward explosion of metal and fire. The force lifted Blanc, throwing him back along the deck. Flame and smoke momentarily engulfed him. Then it was gone. Miraculously, he was unharmed, apart from burns to his uniform and a blackened face. He sat up, shaken by the experience. His hair, beard and moustache were singed too. He patted some small flame out from his beard. Blanc was dazed and perplexed and tried to gather his confused wits. Around him lay lumps of metal debris. Miraculously, all had missed him. He stared around in astonishment. Pandemonium was everywhere; seamen were rushing here, there and everywhere. He looked back to where he had been standing. To his utter amazement, he saw there was a huge scorched hole in the metal hulk. A colossal cavity in the iron-cladding that extended from the water line up to the main deck where he was. It was as though part of the metal hull had melted away, like a thin layer of ice. The hissing of sea water against the scorched metal sent up a flurry of steam. Internal explosions could be heard from within the decks of F.S. *Ney*.

And the young lieutenant was gone.

The officer had been standing right within the damaged cavity left by the heat ray. Anxiously, the old quartermaster looked about for him. Then he accepted the unfortunate man was gone. Blown to oblivion, while he, standing a few feet away, had survived. He looked up, still dazed. The fleet's big guns were blazing away despite the hit. F.S. *Ney* continued throwing more defiant shells, along with the rest of the international fleet.

Ever increasing and more concentrated explosions erupted upon the shore, forcing the last injured and burning fighting machine to move about, wearily trying to dodge the salvo like a punch-drunk boxer. It still managed to discharge bolts of heat ray into the convoy. But the shots were now less frequent. The burning machine seemed to stagger. Blanc gritted his teeth and clenched his fist.

"Fall, you Martian bastard," he muttered.

His dirty face beamed with beautiful and wicked triumph. He watched the second of the hideous machines wobble amid a forest of flaming explosions. Blanc savoured every moment, delighting in the new upsurge of Earth. Like a tree trunk of soil growing instantly, then flaming foliage blossomed. The burning uproar engulfed the fighting machine. It smashed the broken monstrosity, which staggered about the angry, erupting earth. A glorious man-made Hell that brought a taste of vengeance to the Martians. The crippled fighting machine managed to retreat. The titanic alien contraption lumbered away into the darkness of the abandoned country, a dystopian land covered by night, and away from the fires of angry humanity.

The F.S. *Ney*'s internal explosions grew in intensity and the giant vessel listed to port. It was obvious sea water was flooding the lower decks at frightening speed. But the ship's guns still roared away defiantly at the coastline. Lending her last gasps of life to the combined effort of human ants that were fixed upon their goal. Kill the Martians – they can die – they will die – everything must end.

The call to abandon ship was signalled, and seamen began making for the lifeboats. Everything was happening so fast – the ship was lost and the tons of metal that had been breached gave the vessel no chance. She was doomed, and all who stayed with her would be too. But the ship's guns were still firing. In spite of everything, there were men inside the turrets labouring to keep the big guns going.

Amid the mayhem, Blanc struggled to stand. He was shocked by the enormity of the damage witnessed. And in awe of the stubborn men who remained at the big guns inside the revolving turrets. They were seamen made of a very special mettle. Once again, he turned his amazed attention upon the coastline. There was no let-up in the frantic bombardment, even though both fighting machines were spent. One destroyed, the other fleeing inland trailing fire. Lavish bombardment continued to rain down upon the shore, and from out of the tortured landscape the heat rays were coming no more. The international fleet continued stubbornly to deliver fire and metal. The two tripods had managed to destroy three ships, in Blanc's estimation. One of them was F.S. *Ney*.

The spell of his awe-inspired gaze was broken by shouts from a small group of sailors in a nearby lifeboat. Earnestly, they implored him to get aboard as the small craft was being lowered into the sea.

"Quickly sir, there is not much time, it will go down," a friendly voice called from the small lifeboat crew.

The quartermaster staggered along the tilting deck towards the descending lifeboat. He jumped the short distance down onto the suspended craft, and landed among the frightened sailors. Firm hands grabbed him as he almost lost his footing, preventing him from going over the side. The suspended lifeboat rocked as the men steadied him. They continued to lower the boat. It hit the choppy sea as the ropes were released from the pulleys. The crew instantly began to row away from the crippled and burning F.S. *Ney*. The battleship was finished. They all knew. The burning wreck continued to list, amid the shouts of desperate sailors still aboard.

Blanc looked out across the water towards the land bathed in the light of a man-made inferno. He could just make out the opening of the River Crouch's mouth, leading inland to the south of the pulverising bombardment of the international fleet. From the northern side of the estuary the Martian tripods had been dispatched. He and the lifeboat crew were eager to leave Holliwell Point.

"There are no Martian reinforcements," said Blanc amid the diminishing booms of the onward moving fleet. There would be no ship stopping for survivors.

"This is no longer unusual," replied Lefebvre, one of the sailors gripping an oar.

"Perhaps they realised there were more ships then they could match?" added another seaman, Dubois.

Blanc nodded his head and muttered. "Our giant man-made machines are manoeuvrable upon the sea. The sea is too deep for the machines to walk."

"There are rumours of flying Martian machines," said a nervous young seaman. Blanc recognised the youngster as Bisset. The old quartermaster was pleased the youngster had got away.

"Rumours, yes." Blanc smiled and then added reassuringly. "I have yet to see or hear of anyone who actually has seen such a machine."

A seasoned sailor named Laurent spoke next. "This is a more frequent story now. The Martian tripods cannot muster in great numbers anymore. The reports must be true. These Martians are becoming ill. There is something wrong with them. We could never have fought them like this before."

Blanc looked at the southern shore of the river mouth and decided they should make for a landing just down the river along that particular bank. They were at the tail end of the convoy and no ship could or would stop for them. He was the senior ranking man in the boat, and the men needed his decisiveness to feel secure. This he could do, and with firm authority. He instructed them according to his thoughts.

"We must row down the estuary and cling to the opposite bank. We will find a place to go ashore in time."

His men complied and rowed vigorously towards the southern opening at Foulness Point. A huge explosion from the listing F.S. *Ney* momentarily forced each man to freeze in horror. They watched as the grand central battery ship was engulfed in a ball of violent and torrid flame. The heart-breaking spectacle played out before them as the iron inferno capsized and was devoured by the frothing and angry sea.

"Oh my God! The *Ney* has gone," Dubois muttered sadly.

"Yes," agreed Blanc. "*Ney* is gone." He looked to the seamen before him and needed to emphasise: "But we are very much alive, my men. We must try to keep things so."

They continued to row towards the barely visible river mouth. Blanc looked up, knowing that the morning light would soon be upon them. What new horrors awaited them in the coming day? Thank God he could speak English. It would be very useful. "There must be people in hiding. We'll find shelter and survivors. That will be our priority."

The French lifeboat crew rowed into the estuary of the River Crouch, putting distance between them and the onward moving fleet. The craft was full and they had not searched for survivors. Nor had they seen or heard any. The instructions were to keep moving. If there were other lifeboat crews, they would be making for the English shore too. No one from the fleet would be looking for them. Everyone in the small craft wanted to reach the shore, or at least get into the river and away from the sea, Martians or not. The survivors reasoned that they might evade the fighting machines by hiding.

Gradually, the bombardment of fleet action ceased. The line of shipping passed on.

"There will be more tripods inland," Blanc said to the crew of survivors. "For us all, a new ordeal begins."

"We only have a few firearms, sir," said Laurent.

"I would think there will be discarded weaponry on shore. There have been army units wiped out everywhere. However, I think our best defence will be to hide, and when we do move, it must be with stealth," Blanc replied firmly.

There were murmurs of agreement from the men in the boat, and the oars slapped into the sea and pushed them forward towards the darker side of the eerie landscape. They rowed on into the engulfing blackness of the night, away from the burning shore of Holliwell Point on the northern shoreline of the estuary. Another, distant, vessel burning out at sea – another victim of the Martian heat rays.

The Last Days of the Fighting Machine

The muted lifeboat crew targeted their dark section of coastline with reluctant but acceptable zeal. Slowly but surely their small vessel approached the dark shoreline. As they entered the mouth of the River Crouch, the burning landscape to the north cast a stronger glow upon their intended southern bank. Red-tinged vegetation glowed in the flickering illumination. The water had calmed by the time the sailors entered the estuary.

"That red weed," muttered Lefebvre, observing the vegetation as the light flickered over it. "It is more of a sickly pink. It seems to be losing it redness."

"Perhaps it is dying?" replied Blanc. "The way our vegetation does in autumn?"

Lefebvre pondered Blanc's words for a moment. It made some sense. But then he shook his head. "It could be, but I do not think so. I think it is dying. I think all Martian life is dying. Including the abominations in their fighting machines."

Blanc smiled. "Well, that is an encouraging thought. I'm sure we all hope you are right."

There was a nervous and hushed chuckle from the frightened sailors. The tension eased a little.

Dubois asked: "Has anyone ever seen a Martian? I don't mean the machines. I mean the things inside them. I've heard people speak of three-legged beings. Their legs have three toes or fingers and they can use these legs as arms, hands or feet. Is this true?"

Blanc nodded his head. "I have heard they have three legs too. But most of this is hearsay. Maybe we'll meet English people when we get ashore. They will be able to tell us."

"I have seen the fighting machines close up through the binoculars and in daylight," said Laurent. "It was during that offshore engagement we had two days ago."

All turned to Laurent. Some had heard his description before and muttered comments of support.

"Yes, Laurent saw them through the big compound porthole that looks like a window," said Dubois. "Tell them, Laurent. Tell them what you saw."

"Well," began the young seaman. "It was a quick glimpse, but it was not clear. The green port hole was misty but I'm sure there were two of the creatures looking out of the strange window. They looked like giant cauliflowers with huge black eyes and tentacles. Like the sort of oval eyes you see on a grasshopper. But they were big. There was also a giant beak on each of these cauliflower things. The sort of shape we would see on a bird."

Blanc frowned. "Giant cauliflowers with multiple tentacles with giant grasshopper eyes and a giant sparrow's beak? What happened to the three legs?"

"Oh, I think they have three legs and then the tentacles too," answered Laurent, a little nervously as he rowed.

Blanc raised an enquiring eyebrow. "And you saw this through the misty green port hole of a fighting machine?"

"Yes sir. That is exactly how I would describe what I saw. I could not make out three legs. But there were lots of arms. I have even heard people say the Martians have tentacles like those of an octopus. I noticed shadows that looked like such things. But I only got a quick glimpse. Their fighting machines have an array of tentacles and they have three legs. Perhaps the Martians designed the machines the way they actually look. After all, the fighting machine walks on three legs and has an array of tentacles."

"I've heard they suck blood," said Lefebvre. "I'm certain that is true. I met an English refugee at Cherbourg. He said he saw such a thing."

Blanc raised another eyebrow. "What, this Englishman saw a Martian sucking people's blood?"

"No," replied Lefebvre knowledgeably. "He saw the Martians doing such things to sheep. He was hiding in a wood. The sheep were lifted off the ground via the tentacle that the machines have. The terrified animals were put inside a basket thing at the back of the tripod. When this Englishman spoke of it with others, he was told they also do it to people. Martians will suck the blood of anything they can catch."

Again, silence descended upon the lifeboat crew. Each began to imagine the dreadful land they were about to enter. Britain was virtually quarantined. It was a cage full of alien blood suckers, and they were entering this cage.

Each sailor felt the ominous knotting of dread in the pit of his stomach. They were entering a world that was intolerant of humans. None spoke anymore, not even a whisper. The little boat ploughed through the river, hugging the land bank to the south. Some peered toward the burning northern shore, where they knew a dead tripod lay amid the consuming flames. Thankfully, for the moment there was no further signs of the dreaded fighting machines. The second abomination had fled inland.

Blanc looked east, beyond the stern of the boat, and could see the dim red radiance of sky along the horizon. Morning would soon be upon them and it would not be wise to be caught in the open river during daylight. He made out another river inlet along the southern land mass and whispered to the rowers to make for it.

Laurent suddenly lowered his binoculars. With a concerned look he handed them to Blanc, and pointed to the west. "There is something moving a few miles up the river on the northern side. It is barely visible. But I think it is the tripod that fled the engagement. It is some distance off but I'm sure it is heading back in this direction."

Blanc took the binoculars as everyone in the boat hushed. The anticipation was dreadful, a silence that gnawed at each man's anxious soul.

"My God!" Blanc replied. "I think it is crippled. The thing is leaking smoke. It looks injured."

"Yes," agreed Laurent. "It is a long way off, but it seems to be staggering this way."

Dubois was fearful and perplexed. "How can you see in that blackness? Are you sure? Do you think it has seen us?"

"It has been in the battle," Blanc answered. "I doubt that it has seen us. Let us get to the shoreline on the south side. We'll keep hidden. It will not be long now. The daylight will be upon us soon. We need to be able to hide."

The boat went into the still creek. Only the sound of the oars slapping the calm, dirty waters broke the uninviting silence of the dawn. A mist hovered above the stream. On either side, muddy banks rose towards turf that was a confusion of natural green battling the ailing, pink vegetation. The whole spectacle was uncanny, and the French naval crew stared on in astonished silence. They wondered what had become of the rich, green English landscape. It was as though they were rowing their boat on some alien planet where the plant life was a sickly pink. The way one might imagine Mars to be.

"We must get ashore and make our way inland," added Blanc. "We'll find shelter and try to hold out. I think the reports of the Martians dying are true. Hopefully, we will just need to bide our time. We keep hidden and let nature or the elements take their course. Something is causing these alien things problems. This is apparent. All we need to do is lay low for a while."

Murmurs of agreement followed. It was a sound idea. Keep out of the way and let the blasted Martians die in their own way.

CHAPTER 2

THE CONSTABLE OF CANEWDON

The navel bombardment had woken P.C. Adrian Llewellyn. He had shot upright from his bed in his dark sanctuary. Instantly, the lone policeman got up. He groped about in the dark for his uniform trousers and quickly pulled them on over his long johns and adjusted his braces. He then grabbed his police jacket. He wanted to light a candle, but refrained. He was secluded in the cellar, inside the station's prison cell – requisitioned by him for his own use. Safe and below ground, in pitch black, how welcome the darkness was. How dreadful was the daylight.

"No candles," he muttered. "Not after last time."

Even though the gunners were human, they would be firing at the alien tripods and he could not risk being near light. The Martians would respond to any sign. This new development was bringing back memories of the previous months.

The aliens had been roaming the countryside at will and constantly. Llewellyn had almost been caught when Martian tentacles had smashed through the station window one night. He had been working by candle light at the front desk. The windows had been covered, but the Martians seemed to know he was there. He had got to the cellar door, where stairs led down to the prison cells. Frightened beyond reason, Llewellyn managed to shut and bolt the cellar door. He had gone down and locked himself inside a prison cell. The alien machine's tentacle smashed through the locked door. The fear had been almost unbearable. He remembered the Martian war cry of "*Ulla*" screaming out in the night.

He cursed the memory of that alien cry. That call had often been heard in the night, but usually it was far off. This night it had been very close. Llewellyn shuddered at the memory. Now he had heard the Martians again. This time they were up against the navies of the world. The Martians were fighting a war for the world, and they appeared to be losing. He was certain of it. Something had gone seriously wrong with them. They were less numerous. Recently, he had gone a whole day without seeing or hearing a fighting machine. It had been encouraging. Yet this night had brought a few into the area. Albeit on the other side of the River Crouch, where he supposed Burnham-on-Crouch might be.

"You alien boyos will not go quietly though, will you," he fumed, hoping an all-knowing, all-seeing godly entity might be watching protectively over him.

"Christ, I thought they had gone," Llewellyn cursed in the darkness, kicking the bed post. He tried to refocus on the present and shake off the dreadful thoughts of alien fighting machines. He took courage from the thought that organised human activity was close at hand. It also filled him with curiosity. He had heard guns in the distance before. But this bombardment was much closer than usual. He had not heard fighting this close for a long time. This meant the presence of the terrifying Martian fighting machines, but also of humanity. Humanity, that still had guns, close by. And above all, something was wrong with the Martians!

"They have changed," muttered Llewellyn. "There are not so many. I can't say why, but I know something is wrong with these abominations. The red weed is dying too. It is turning sickly pink, and looks rank."

Llewellyn's encouragement grew as the ground shook from the distant explosions across the river. He picked up his helmet. Why he continued to work the police station was beyond him. But he could not think of anything better to do. He put the helmet on and pulled the strap neatly under his chin. Then he left the sanctuary of the prison cell and to go upstairs.

"God blast it," he fumed as he tripped and fell on the first step. It was pitch black, and in his excitement he had miscalculated. "I should have bloody well left with the rest of them." He looked up at the ceiling and pulled a face of disdain for the hidden Almighty. He believed God was watching over him. "Perhaps you are having a little chuckle," he said light-heartedly. "I might have been long out of all this mess." Then he thought of the probable millions who had been slaughtered as they had fled the cities *en masse*. He might have been one of those if he had not decided to wait for orders. Llewellyn laughed at himself. "What a pathetic silly sod I am. Nowhere without orders! Orders from where? Still, such foolhardy notions and indecisiveness has kept me alive."

He looked up at the ceiling, certain that the Almighty was looking down at him. "I'm alive because I'm a fool who needs to be instructed all the time. But right now, I'm not knocking it."

Llewellyn was carrying his boots and socks, tiptoeing up the stairs through the pitch black of the underground area. He winced nervously as he trod on the cold stone floor at the top. Before him was the locked door that led to the police station at ground level. He fumbled about and found the bolt. The loud clang of the lock sliding back made him wince. Everything sounded louder in darkness. This upper part of the building was as murky as the cellar, but he knew the place was tidy from his constant attentions over the past two weeks. With his usual proficiency, P.C. Llewellyn had made the station look as normal as it had in peacetime – before the invasion of the Martians.

Warily, he made his way through the gloom towards the desk. There was a set of binoculars in the top draw. Groping around in the darkness, he found it. His eyes were becoming accustomed to the darkness as he made his way towards one of the windows. He opened the wooden shutters that kept out the night air. The window frames were missing their glass panes. They had been smashed during the earlier tripod search. All that had happened weeks back. Llewellyn had cleaned up the debris and restored some form of order to the station.

"Why I stay, I'll never know," he muttered to God. P.C. Llewellyn had taken to talking to God of late. He had become a more avid believer since losing faith when the first part of the tribulation had come to the remote corner of Essex. He wondered if the tripods had got as far as his place of birth, in

Swansea. He shuddered at the thought of the gigantic tripods walking across his beloved Welsh valleys.

As the cool, night air brushed his face, his eyes widened. To the east, the distant horizon glowed red. The light of dawn was helped by the burning desolation. The bombardment had stopped and he could not see any silhouettes of the alien tripods moving in his direction. He raised the binoculars to his eyes.

"Where is the Martian bastard?" he muttered. "Have the ships got one?"

He lowered the binoculars and looked around to his rear. He could not see other tripods coming. He strained to hear the battle cry of "*Ulla*" but there was nothing.

"Too hot for you lot, eh boyos?" A grin spread across his cherubic face, and his long thin moustache turned upwards at the ends towards his ears.

Then he heard the sound of a far-off tripod's thumping footfall. It was not from the direction of the burning. The sound was coming from the north-west.

Llewellyn raised his binoculars and peered into the gloomy night. He could make out trees on the other side of the River Crouch. Then he made out the distant motion of a tripod. It was just visible in the first tinge of dawn light, taking enormous steps across the blackened trees along the opposite bank of the river.

"Another bastard," Llewellyn scoffed to God, his one true companion of late. "This one's injured. The bastard looks as though it is limping. Bloody marvellous. The bugger is trailing black smoke. A shell must have hit a part that contains the poisonous black smoke. The canisters must have ruptured. It is causing the smoke to leak out. If it was at the shoreline, it must have retreated and is now arcing about in this direction. Therefore, it must have been wounded at the shore and wandered inland before circling about." He sighed to himself. God never answered via speaking. It was the way of things with God.

Suddenly, he froze with the realisation that the poisonous smoke could spread. If it did not have time to thin, the wind could blow the cloud towards the police station. Llewellyn shuddered at the thought. He would surely choke to death on the fumes. The fighting machine was a long way off, but Llewellyn was exceptionally paranoid of late.

"Oh bugger," he cursed, and he ran back to the desk and grabbed his keys. Why he felt the need for his keys, he did not know.

"I've got to get away."

He pulled out his handkerchief and ran bare foot out into the summer night, making for the coal bunker. There was a bowl of stagnant water close by. He plunged his handkerchief into it and grabbed a lump of coal from the bunker, wrapping it in the wet rag. He had heard that if someone breathed through damp coal then the effects of the smoke would not be severe if you were on the fringes of the cloud. He had not put it to the test, but had heard the tale from passers-by at Maldon some months back during the HMS *Thunder Child* battle of the Blackwater.

For a moment, he stopped to consider the people he had seen after the events at Maldon. None had wanted to stay at Canewdon. They had all decided to disperse and take their chances. Many journeyed back inland once they knew the Martians had reached the coastlines. It was as though everyone was running to find a good hiding place.

The great Martian machine came lumbering through the murky night along the opposite side of the river. Llewellyn's heart started to pound with fear. He hid by the coal bunker, his binoculars firmly fixed upon the machine trailing its thinning black smoke. Even in the darkness, there was enough firelight from the distant burning coast to perceive the rupture on the side of its body trunk. The hydraulic joints creaked as the machine moved, and it was obvious the Martian machine was damaged.

Ullugh!

The deep sound reverberated across the night. Llewellyn thought it might be a distress call. It was unusual, for the machines usually came to each other's aid. As the policeman scanned the entire area, he could make out no assistance.

"This is getting stranger by the day," he whispered to himself. "First, they seem to become scarce, as though uninterested in exploring and searching for people, and now they abandon their wounded. Oh, great almighty God, what is going on?"

The first signs of dawn began to clear the eastern horizon. Streaks of light were cast upon the lumbering tripod's body. Groves and gullies glinted upon the dirty off-white construction, and reflective sparkles flickered upon the compound port hole window. Llewellyn also made out the shaded form of some globular-looking creature. A giant onion-shaped shadow. Tendrils seemed to come from its lumpish form. Perhaps it was working a control system that drove the machine. It was the merest glimpse as the strange window section became obscured again – hidden by what still remained of the darkness.

The alien vehicle's thunderous steps shook the earth as it came closer to the river. Suddenly, its tall frame sank behind a line of trees. Llewellyn realised the machine had stepped into the River Crouch and its huge limbs sank into the river bed. His heart skipped a beat. He sprang back in fear when he heard the huge splash of displaced water tearing out through the dawn. For a terrifying moment, he thought that the machine was coming for him. He ran back into the police station. He slammed the door before sneaking to the open shutters, which he quickly closed. He stayed put and stared through the small crack in the shutters. His teeth were chattering, and his body was at the point of convulsion. He tried to get a grip on his fear, a pulsating horror that invaded his entire person. The alarm of seeing the tripod come back into view helped him. The machine had crossed the River Crouch in a few giant steps. The surprise of its re-emergence distracted his inner fear to a cold sweat. His shaking had stopped, and he was just frozen to the spot.

The machine took a giant stride up onto the southern side of the river bank, where the deserted little village of Canewdon lay – the abode of Llewellyn and also his police station.

"Oh my God!"

Llewellyn yelped as he pressed the damp handkerchief and the black coal to his mouth. His heart was thumping away again. Inside he felt his chest tightening. Despite the intense fear he still could not tear himself away from the window-shutter's crack, even though he was telling himself he would be safer down stairs in the cells.

A huge leg crashed down in the open grass between the small station and the trees. Amid

The Last Days of the Fighting Machine

the sound of loud creaking alloy, the body trunk moved unsteadily forward. Another long appendage crashed to the side, while the third came down in front of the tree line, allowing the colossal thing to balance. The tripod looked uncertain on its legs, and Llewellyn could see that it was more cumbersome than others he had observed. He assumed it was due to damage it had sustained. For a moment it lingered, as though pondering what it should do next. Once again, Llewellyn made out the grotesque, globular shadow within the compound window structure. With the thin tendrils coming from the body shape, it was like a blurred image of a giant spider behind a net.

Llewellyn shuddered. He wondered if the thing would fumble around the station with its tentacle sensors, things that hissed and whipped around the body structure. He had seen the long, thin feelers pick up people and sheep.

Slowly, he lowered the damp handkerchief from his coal blackened mouth and frowned. He looked up at the ruptured alloy on the side of the machine. There was no more black smoke pouring out of the shell hole. The black substance was exhausted. For what seemed like a long time, the tripod stood motionless. More of the morning light began to fan out across the sky. Llewellyn drank in the awesome sight of the giant machine. The off-white alloy of the machine's metal legs had huge external veins or pipes that had twisted about the limbs like some parasitical plant. These vein-like conduits were massed and concentrated around the leg's hydraulic joints. Each of its three limbs were raised up and inwards towards the body trunk. The vessel that contained Martian or Martians was high above, the alien safety encasement tank.

Llewellyn had never seen the actual Martian creatures. Nor had he ever wanted to. Now was the closest he had come to fathoming what the blurred silhouette might be. This remained a distorted approximation through the misty compound window construction.

For a morbid moment he studied the colossal alien vehicle. A giant edifice against the dawn sky. The protective trunk resembled a giant onion with a circular compound window. There were other smaller openings. These were transparent with haze too. Perhaps spy holes? No one knew what the substance was, but Llewellyn guessed it was not glass. It had to be something stronger. A green radiance glowed from within. It looked like a hard resin. The bulbous alien creature's outline was visible again, a distorted silhouette in the green haze. The huge container had the appearance of a one-eyed insect's head. Small trap doors remained open beneath the undercarriage of the trunk. The flexible tentacles

The Last Days of the Fighting Machine

dropped down and waved about between the giant machine's legs, like a bunch of agitated hissing serpents.

Llewellyn's breathing was laboured. He put a hand to his thumping chest, battling with this sweating fear. His resolve was weakening. He began to dread the worst. Perhaps the fighting machine intended to search the premises with him inside? He would surely be discovered. He moved away from the join of the shutters, and leaned against the wall. Breathing through his nose and out via his mouth, he was slowly trying to win the inner battle against gnawing phobia.

Llewellyn looked to the cellar door. The beautiful stairs were beyond, welcome steps that went down into the dark sanctuary. The repaired door, which could be locked. For a moment, he considered going back down to his hidden cell. But he knew from past experience the tentacle sensors could get down there. The building had been searched some six weeks back during the height of the tripod activity. His memories of cowering beneath the bed, while the scaled metal protuberance had rummaged around the prison cell, came back to haunt him. He dismissed the notion. His resolve was slowly returning. A small part of him was winning the inner battle. The concoction of resolution and past terror caused him to remain still and frozen – that past memory of an alien feeler moving around his motionless, prostrate body. He reasoned that he might as well do the same by the wall next to the window if the tentacles entered the police station again. After all, the feeler went for all the obscure places where one might hide and he knew he had to remain still. Try not to panic under any circumstance.

"That was the trick," he whispered to himself. "Never move. Never lose control of yourself."

He took a deep breath, expecting the shutters to smash in at any moment. Would the alien machinery come into the station? The time dragged agonisingly on. The suspense began to tear away. He could feel layers of his resolve being peeled away.

"Why has it not happened?" he hissed.

Was the Martian toying with him? He wondered what the wretched things were like hidden within their huge tripod vehicles. Do the Martians reason cruelly? What are the monsters' devious ways of flushing a person out of a building?

"The machine has no black smoke," he reasoned to himself. A small twinge of relief. The Martian would not be able to fumigate the area and drive him out, exposed, choking and spluttering into the waiting tentacles – where he would be lifted and displayed before the green window orb. Legs kicking, mouth screaming in terror. Just prior to the huge and wicked syringes of the monstrous technology – the plungers that would pierce him first. He cringed and winced at the dreadful thought. The memory of past victims. Human and sheep. The spasmodic fits of the helpless victims as the injection went in. The solution or venom that caused the terrible shaking and screaming for a few seconds. Then the limpness of being paralysed as the body was drained of blood. Consumed while still alive. Open-mouthed horror as the victim's eyes went sickly white. The irises gone under the upper socket. Staring up into the brain and skull.

He shuddered at the thought. Just white sclera in sunken dead eye sockets.

"Oh God!" he hissed, and tried to drive the thoughts out of his mind. He had been living like a rat in a lair. Being a safe rat was all right. A live rat was good. Better a live rat than a dead one. Moment by moment, he came down from the height of his trepidation.

Nothing had happened.

After a while, he began to gingerly move back towards the shutters. Maybe the Martian wanted him to do this and it was part of its waiting game. If so, he was playing right into the Martian's tentacles. But Llewellyn could no longer continue his waiting. He had to see if he could spot an advantage. A risk had to be taken. His eye drifted across the tiny gap between the closed shutters. His unease was instantly abated. The tentacles of the fighting tripod machine were working upon the knee joint of one of the huge alloyed legs. It was trying to repair itself. Unwinding a huge fastener upon the hydraulics of the elevated intersection.

The Martian was not looking for him. Suddenly better judgement began to yield reassurance. Llewellyn grew in confidence as he watched from his place of concealment. He wondered about the Martian or Martians inside the huge mechanical tool. In reality, he had only ever seen the huge fighting apparatus the Martians used. Now he had some perception of a creature inside the machine. The enormous conveyance on huge, ungainly legs that spat heat and poisonous smoke was a mere vehicle. What did the things inside look like? He shuddered at how they might appear and imagined green, slimy creatures oozing foul mucus from all parts of their anatomy.

Why?

Llewellyn supposed all people wanted to think of something foul. He had never seen or heard from anyone who had seen a Martian up close. For all his terrified imaginings, the actual Martian being remained an enigma to him.

Ulla!

The roar shook the ground and the very air. The ear-splitting screech reverberated and fanned out across the fields and into the police station.

The Last Days of the Fighting Machine

The fighting machine moved forward and stepped over the police complex. Llewellyn gulped and ran across the room to the shutters on the other side. Joyous relief swelled as the alien titan strode southwards, over the countryside and away from the deserted village of Canewdon. After a few long strides, it veered off eastwards.

"It's moving towards Wallasea Island," he muttered. His eyes widened in concern. "Oh God! Paglesham Churchend! Mrs Steed and her son were hiding there. I will have to go there."

This change of direction. The Martian fighting machine had given rise to a new set of circumstances. Llewellyn was still a policeman, and he must still function as one. Even under such dire conditions.

"You don't sound well, boyo," he cursed at the fighting machine. "Let's hope it is something serious."

He watched with mounting concern as the huge tripod strode across the fields towards the little village of Paglesham Churchend.

"The Martian inside must have seen the church tower. God, of all places why Paglesham? Never was a place as remote as that little village. It is why Mrs Steed had stayed there with her simple son, Reggie, and her grandson."

Morning light began to fill the small room. Llewellyn started to shake with a new and different fear. He was also excited. He had made his decision.

He would have to go to Paglesham Churchend to aid Mrs Steed. She would need help and he had not a moment to lose. He looked towards the fat diary he had been painstakingly keeping during his isolation at Canewdon.

"I must make a written report before I set off," he grumbled to himself. The notes he had kept on a day to day basis had kept him going, and if anything should happen to him, he wanted the constabulary to know that he had done what he considered his duty. Despite the most testing of times anyone could have ever envisaged, P.C. Llewellyn would do his duty to the very best of his ability.

He grabbed his pen and quickly began to scribble down the recent events.

P.C. Adrian Llewellyn 31st August 1898

> *As mentioned earlier I cycled out to Paglesham Churchend and been very pleasantly surprised to discover that Mrs Steed had remained in her cottage, despite the rest of the village evacuating their homes. She was with her son Reginald and her grandson Jimmy, the child of her deceased daughter. Reggie is about thirty years of age but is afflicted by learning difficulties, and has the mind*

of a young boy. I have just watched a Martian fighting machine make its way towards the village where they are hiding.

Mrs Steed and her family will be in great danger. I am going to Paglesham Churchend to be of assistance to her in this new and terrible situation. So far, Mrs Steed is the only person I have discovered in the course of my rounds since I started to venture back outside. Things had been going quietly until the naval action last night. I think the Martians were engaged across the river to the north-east. One machine was crippled and it appeared this morning. It has a shell hole to its side. I think this happened during the battle. It approached from the east, but I think it is circling about in some form of confusion. It has now gone towards the village of Paglesham Churchend after crossing the river near Canewdon. I am concerned for the safety of Mrs Steed and her family, and I am going to Paglesham Churchend. If some ill befalls me during this, please note that I did my duty as a policeman to the bitter end.

God Save the Queen.

⇌ ⇋

Quickly, Llewellyn pulled on his socks and boots. Then he grabbed his binoculars and went outside to scrub himself in the rain-water bucket he had set up with a barrel via the guttering. His nose wrinkled at the sight of the pink moss. It had been red up until a week ago. Even around the yard, he noticed that green grass and various natural weeds were reclaiming areas that the red weed had occupied. With a sigh of satisfaction, he buttoned his uniform and slung the strap of the binoculars across his shoulder. He looked every part the peacetime country bobby as he walked across the back yard where he had first seen the giant tripod approach. He stopped before his little shed.

Upon opening the shed door, Llewellyn pulled out his bicycle and put on his bicycle clips. With some dignity, he wheeled the bicycle forward. One foot upon the bike pedal while the other foot pushed for momentum – the way all policemen had been taught at the training school. As the bike gathered motion, Llewellyn slung his free leg over the rear wheel and onto the other free peddle. Firmly settling his ample rear upon the soft leather saddle, he set off. He made his way up the dry mud path towards the river, a good old British bobby going about his rounds, but in an apocalyptic landscape where sickly pink weed clung to the hedgerows. The red Martian parasitical plant definitely looked as though it was dying. The policeman even began to whistle as he went about his daily work.

The Last Days of the Fighting Machine

"I'll approach Paglesham Churchend via the river," he said to God. God was back in favour again.

Llewellyn had to steer the bicycle around the indentations of the machine's huge footprint. When he got to the bank of the River Crouch, he stopped.

Making a small effort to keep concealed, he took his binoculars and surveyed the opposite bank. The dawn light was getting brighter. He scanned the horizon for any more tripods. To his relief, there were none. His vision swept along the river up towards the estuary by Wallasea Island.

"Oh, my word!"

The policeman was astounded to catch a glimpse of what looked like armed foreign sailors. It was a fleeting sight, as the group of men were obscured by a small rise in the terrain. Llewellyn guessed they must have come up the Crouch by boat and had turned into the River Roach tributary. From there they had come ashore on Wallasea Island and were now moving stealthily over the pink marshland. They would be in trouble if the alien caught sight of them.

He lowered his binoculars and muttered:

"Well, I'll be damned – they must be survivors from the battle last night. They'll need help too if they're foreign. Oh blast! There will be a few things to do today, all right."

With no time to waste, Llewellyn looked back to the station, nervously noticing the distant and damaged tripod receding from view as it strode eastwards towards the village of Paglesham Churchend. Its hideous trunk stood out against the red morning skyline.

He took his bicycle and went through the usual scooting start before nervously mounting the wobbly contraption's accommodating saddle. Then he set off along the country road and across the pink, apocalyptic landscape. The excited bobby had a half-baked sense of purpose. How that purpose might be fulfilled was beyond him for the moment. He would have to make it up as he went along, and as circumstances dictated. With ill-deserved confidence, P.C. Llewellyn was going into action, a moral British bobby with his policeman's whistle and perhaps a nervous prayer.

CHAPTER 3

MAD DOGS AND ENGLISHMEN

Lewis the poacher scratched his long sharp nose and ran his fingers through his scruffy white hair and beard. From the copse where he had skilfully concealed himself amid the pink and green foliage, the old rogue raised his binoculars. He had acquired them from a dead soldier of a slaughtered army unit some weeks back. He also acquired the rifle and ammunition pouches. There was a great deal of ammunition. His army backpack also contained outdoor essentials. Next to him, a little terrier dog sat, obediently panting away.

Using the illicit skills of his trade, Lewis found hiding and travelling across the red alien landscape second nature. Martian tripods were considerably easier to evade than gamekeepers. In some ways, he had adapted before the Martians fell upon the land.

Gazing out through the eerie mist upon the still morning waters of the River Crouch, he could just make out the opposite bank where the gun salvos and thunderous explosions could be heard during the previous night. In the darkness he had seen the ghostly effigies of giant moving structures. Then he had observed the inferno as the two tripods tried to engage the huge navy from the exposed shore. The star shells illuminated them. There was the joy of one unearthly machine going down. The monstrous tripod limbs had buckled amid the inferno raining down. He had thrilled at the sight of the Martian dying, falling into the flames of a man-made hell. Now it was the Martian's experiencing hell on earth! The other machine was limping away, trailing smoke. Now it had crossed the River Crouch and circled back on the opposite side. His side.

"I could watch those bastards die for hours, Gippy, and never get sick of such a beautiful sight." Lewis grinned at his little terrier, displaying missing front teeth. "I don't care if God does not forgive me. For God must have made these evil bastards too."

Gippy swished her tail as she sat, her only form of reply. The dog never barked. She must have known instinctively. Sometimes she would whine to alert him. But never would she bark.

The ground on the opposite and far-off bank was still burning and smouldering. It sent a tingling sensation of fear into the pit of Lewis' stomach. For a moment all seemed still: the calm, glasslike glaze of the River Crouch; the trees with their unaccustomed, parasitic, pink moss-covered leaves; the absence of early morning birdsong. The only movement was Gippy, sitting beside him and wagging her little tail in her usual contented manner. She was another acquisition, found on his travels. He wondered who her owners had been. Perhaps they were among the estimated millions slaughtered over the past weeks and months. He had shot a few dogs. Many were turning feral, without owners to look after them. Gippy had been different. He had come upon the little mutt at the right time. The terrier had quickly adapted to him as her companion.

Lewis turned his binoculars south where the injured Martian tripod had wandered towards Paglesham Churchend. He had seen the thing cross the river close to Canewdon, the village where he used to live. He had abandoned the place at the beginning of the Martian invasion. After nearly five weeks on a pointless mission to escape with the rest of the population, travelling to coastal towns in the hope of acquiring transport across the sea, now he was trying to make his way back home.

"Aw, my Gawd," muttered Lewis to Gippy. "The other tripod is moving towards Paglesham and Wallasea Island. I wonder if it has seen those foreign sailors. They must have been involved in the bombardment during the night. I suppose they were at Holliwell Point. We got across the river from Burnham just in time, my little old girl."

Gippy whined. She often seemed to utter a low howl. It was her only sound of acknowledgement. Perhaps it was out of respect for the Martian hunters. This was always better than barking. But her little tail always wagged excitedly.

"You're a good little girl, Gippy. When this is all over, you and I will have a great life."

These dreadful days of the Martians would come to an end. "We've seen these derelict monstrosities scattered about the meadows. Crows, ravens and rooks all feasting. These things are dying, Gippy. But some of the buggers are not going quietly."

He stroked the little dog tenderly. Lewis always preferred the company of dogs and cats. They were not as complicated as people.

"Canewdon still seems peaceful," he continued. "We are almost there. Less than a couple of miles." He looked around at the comfortable seclusion. "We'll have to move on soon, Gippy, if we are going to get home while the morning is still here."

The little dog gave a quiet muffled whine, oblivious of the distant Martian's thumping strides.

"No woof, Gippy!" Lewis smiled, then leant forward, adding. "Tripod."

He pointed towards the distant machine lumbering across the fields, moving towards Paglesham Churchend village. "It does seem awful slow. Like it is labouring. Under duress, so to speak. It is only a machine, but the creature inside must be ill. We'll know when the time comes. The carrion will let us know when they flock to it."

Ulla!

As if on cue, and for Gippy's benefit, the Martian call came to them. The hideous noise was almost pitiable. The alien thing sounded different. The wretched moan crossed the pink and green patchwork meadows.

Birds suddenly erupted from the unearthly vegetation in panic. They soared up into the thinning mist, breaking the eerie silence with panic as they scattered in different directions.

"Stay still," whispered Lewis soothingly to the little dog. "It's all right girl, they are going away, but we don't want to attract any attention now do we."

He smiled at the little dog, who responded with a confused and half-hearted wag of her tail. Lewis leant forward and picked up the two dead hares he had snared.

"I think we should leave, little girl. And quietly does it."

He winked at the little terrier and made his way along the covering woodland, down towards the lane. Being a poacher had been in his blood for fifty years now, and he had loved the adventure of it all. The coming of the tripods had given him free licence, though he was not grateful for it. Not by any stretch of the imagination. Capture by tripods would mean a ghastly death, and he shuddered at the memories of the many he had seen captured, when he was trying to flee the country with the rest of humanity at Maldon on the River Blackwater.

He suddenly froze and held a hand out to Gippy. The little dog froze instantly, trusting the old poacher's instincts to the last. In the distance he could hear a faint sound of wheels. Bicycle wheels and somebody whistling. He frowned in confusion amid the ailing pink moss and pale red weed. They looked like plants that are not looked after well and beginning to wither. His surprise jumped to a level of pure astonishment when he heard the humming get louder. For Lewis knew who it would be. He might have guessed. His arch-nemesis, P.C. Llewellyn. Lewis looked down at Gippy and grinned.

"It's all right, girl. Llewellyn is not that bad really. Better him than a Martian."

The policeman on his bicycle was whistling a little tune. He came into view as he rounded a bend, cycling along the red hedgerows towards them. Like an ordinary, everyday bobby in a very unordinary world. His police uniform was a little on the shoddy side, but there the old blighter was, in all his constabulary glory. Going about his usual beat, come what may. Martian tripods and all – a typical bobby, whatever the weather.

Lewis stepped out in the lane with the army rifle over his shoulder in full view of P.C. Llewellyn. Gippy gave a little low-pitched groan and sped off in the direction of the oncoming constable. Lewis could not stop the little mutt.

"Heel, Gippy – heel now."

He walked up the lane after her, continuously trying to make the dog heel. P.C. Lewellyn braked and came to a screeching halt. He wore a big, red, cherubic smile. "Hello there, boy." He leaned down and stroked the little terrier, wagging her tail excitedly.

"She is a little girl," advised Lewis.

For once he was pleased to see the old village bobby. Yet he was totally aghast.

"You been here all the time?" He stopped in front of the constable, totally baffled at the spectacle. "Blooming hell, P.C. Llewellyn. The whole world has gone mad. But that does not seem to stop you from doing your beat."

The old poacher could not contain his mirth. He shook his head in disbelief. A mixture of delight and annoyance. "If you ain't noticed, we've been invaded by monsters from outer space and you still can't take a day off. Are you stark raving mad? Like little Gippy here?" He looked down at his excited mutt and scolded. "Quiet, girl! Quiet, for the sake of my poor mixed up head." He looked around nervously with the rifle still slung over his shoulder, but the tripod was well out of sight.

P.C. Llewellyn regarded Lewis and frowned. "I see I can say the same about you, boyo. Up to your old tricks. Come rain or shine, or even monsters from outer space." His Welsh accent was full of humour, but with a policeman's prying menace.

Lewis nodded a little confession for once. "Such skills have come in handy, I do confess. Let us get into the woods for a moment, it's not safe exposed. I saw some tripod making eastwards moments ago."

"I've taken note of that, Lewis. I've seen it too. I'm trying to get further down the lane. I've seen some sailors further up river. I think they are survivors from the battle last night."

"I've seen them too. They're foreign. I saw the guns and the heat things booming and flashing during the night. I was on that side of the river. Near Burnham-on-Crouch."

Lewis led the way deeper into the woodland, while P.C. Lewellyn followed, lightly slapping his thigh for Gippy to follow. The happy little terrier complied.

"I want to get to the seamen. They might be in need of help." He looked around and then back at

The Last Days of the Fighting Machine

Lewis a little confused. "You're still a little way from Paglesham, your usual poacher's stomping ground."

"I got as far as Harwich. That was after trying my luck at Maldon first. Saw one of the last paddle steamers get out to sea, but only at the cost of a Royal Navy ship. It went up against three tripods."

"The HMS *Thunder Child*." Llewellyn removed his helmet and rubbed sweat from his brow with a handkerchief. A pristine, clean handkerchief. "I heard about that back at Canewdon. Things became intense after that, so I heard." P.C. Llewellyn looked at Lewis, hoping for more information.

The old poacher just shook his head and looked down. "I don't want to go there." He shuddered. "More tripods came, that is all I need to say. I'm sure you would know the rest."

Llewellyn nodded understandably. "All right, boyo, let's let the bad things lay as they are." He looked around for a bit, then turned back. "Have you noticed that there is less movement among the Martians of late? The red weed is dying too."

Lewis confirmed the policeman's theory. "I've thought on this and seen such things too. There are tripods in meadows. Just standing there. Like they are asleep standing up. The carrion are swarming around the top part where the Martians would be. The weed is losing its colour and, apart from last night, the tripods have been scarce. Those I have seen are always lumbering about in the distance. Like the machines are slowing down. Even the one that just passed by seems different. Its movement is slower and unsure. At least, that is how it seems. Something is definitely not right with them. Maybe they have run out of people to eat?"

The Welsh policeman agreed. "I suppose that you are right. Not about the people though. There are still many more in hiding than you might realise. Mrs Steed and her simple son Reggie are still at Paglesham Churchend. She also has that young grandson Jimmy with her too."

"What, Mrs Steed and her mongoloid son …"

"Hush! Don't go using that word to describe Mrs Steed's son, Lewis. Please be careful. Mrs Steed does get terribly upset by the word. She hates that term. So does Jimmy. They both love Reg and are rather offended with how people talk of the man's affliction. The word mongoloid is a definite no-no. Do you understand, Lewis?"

"Well, if you say so P.C. Llewellyn. But what other thing is Reg's condition called?"

"In all honesty, I do not know, except for that term which Mrs Steed hates. Mrs Steed went to some lengths to tell me of a doctor who died a couple of years back. A Doctor Langdon Down from Cornwall, now dead. This doctor made an in-depth study of people like Reg. She refers to it as Down's

Condition because he had done extensive studies concerning this syndrome. It has nothing to do with Mongolian people. Mrs Steed says such comparisons are very ignorant."

Lewis sighed. "I remember she told me about this Doctor Down. But I have never referred to Reggie as mongoloid in front of her, or Reggie. I've even taken Reggie poaching with me. He has aptitude and common sense. Enough to handle a shotgun."

P.C. Llewellyn raised an eyebrow. "Perhaps I did not need to know that, Lewis."

"Sorry, P.C. Llewellyn. I was just trying to say that Reggie's condition is not so extreme."

"Yes, Mrs Steed called it a certain type of learning or development disorder. And that Doctor Down has studied the *syndrome*, I think that is what she called it. Evidently, Reg's condition, according to Doctor Down, is not too extreme. He is slightly backward, but not shockingly so. If you get my meaning."

"Well I know that, P.C. Llewellyn. Reg is a very good poacher."

Llewellyn lifted an eyebrow. "I know. Reg told me he used to go out with you and Mister Walker. He has a gullible innocence."

"Well, if Mrs Steed did lie low during the Martian invasion, Reg would know how to get food off of the land. He can catch pheasants, rabbits and all sorts. The bloke is a natural."

"Well, Mrs Steed has, and our Reg has been teaching Jimmy a thing or two."

Lewis looked shocked. "You have got to be pulling my leg, Sir. Surely Mrs Steed would not have stayed behind." He laughed with joy of such splendid news.

"No, Lewis, I'm not pulling your leg, boyo. Not at all. Mrs Steed endured the Martian tripod searches. She managed to hide when the fighting machines went into to the village. She hid in the church crypt with Reggie and Jimmy. They are now plucky survivalists."

Lewis smiled and shook his head in delighted disbelief. "That stubborn old cow will never budge for anything." There was a hint of admiration in his voice. "She made a wise decision. If she had tried to go to Maldon or Southend, it is likely she would have been killed before getting aboard a boat."

"I'm a bit worried for her now though. I saw that tripod machine trailing smoke. It was going towards Paglesham Churchend."

Lewis looked at the policeman and raised an eyebrow. "That machine has come from the conflict that was going on during the night. Of those two machines, one is dead and the injured one is going to Paglesham Churchend."

Llewellyn nodded in agreement. "The injured one has come over via Canewdon and has now turned in the direction of little Paglesham Churchend. That was the last I saw of it. I've kept a lookout for it coming back and have not seen anything as of yet. I was going to take a trip over there, but I've seen the sailors near the River Roach on Wallasea Island. I thought maybe I could enlist the help of the sailors. They seemed as though they were armed."

"Were they in a life boat then?"

P.C. Llewellyn nodded. "I never saw one, but I'm supposing they left it on the mud bank before venturing over the marshland. Maybe their ship was sunk and they were the only survivors."

Lewis held up his rifle. "I'll go there with you. I would like to see the Steed family. Are there any others that stayed behind?"

"You'll only see the Steeds," Llewellyn replied. "The Walkers were there too, but I'm afraid they were not as cautious as the Steeds."

"How have you come by this information?" Lewis was totally bemused by P.C. Llewellyn and how he had kept in touch with things.

"I've been doing my rounds over the past week. I go to Paglesham Churchend regularly. I tried Paglesham Eastend but there is no one there. Only the dead of an army unit. They got caught there some time back. They did not stand a chance. As you know, the tripods are not as numerous as before. When one does appear, they seem easy enough to avoid."

"What, you mean you've been riding about on your bike amid all of this?" Lewis held out his arms and looked about at the deranged and sickly pink, red and green landscape.

"Well, you've still been out up to your old antics, haven't you now?"

Lewis looked a little embarrassed as he held up the two hares. "Well, I think I can put this down to survival or are you going to pinch me."

Llewellyn chuckled. "Don't be so daft now, I'm sure Her Majesty Queen Victoria will forgive you. And we can find good use for them there hares. Let's push on up river in the meantime. First the seamen who have come ashore. Then to Paglesham to see how Mrs Steed will be getting on."

As P.C. Llewellyn left the woods and went back into the lane, Lewis and Gippy followed, happy to be around someone else.

"I almost feel sorry for the Martians if they meet Mrs Steed. She can be a bit scary sometimes," Lewis joked. The old bridle path's shingle crunched beneath their footsteps.

Changing the subject, Llewellyn enquired: "So what have you been doing with yourself over the past weeks, Lewis?" He smiled. "Been bottled up like the rest of us, have you?"

"That's putting it mildly. I decided to come back after getting nowhere at Harwich. Maldon was no go beforehand, as I said. I just made my way back." Lewis shook his head in wonder at the memory of his return journey. "What disturbing and eerie sights I've seen on my journey back. The Essex meadows all awash in red weed, and those strange machines, just standing around for the most part. I thought they had started to hibernate or something like that. Most of them had just seemed to stop. Sometimes there was the odd one lumbering about. They look like they're drunk. Great big machines that are ill. Then they just stop. Most of them were miles away. I never went near them. I always gave them a wide birth. They never moved, just standing there. Always crows and rooks flying overhead, not scared of them at all. That's why I think that many of the machines were dead. Carrion only go near things that are dead and rotting."

Llewellyn raised an eyebrow. "Well, I hope you're right about that, Lewis. That is very encouraging. Very encouraging indeed."

"Little Gippy and I only plucked up the nerve to go out over the past few days. I ended up at Latchingdon, and then went to Althorne. I stayed there for a few days. Great views of the estuary from Althorne. The sight of the red meadows gradually going pink as the green starts to come back was uplifting. I could see the difference over the four days I stayed in Althorne. Then a deserted cottage near Burnham, and it was only hunger that drove me to move on. Little Gippy and I got across the Crouch last night in a rowing boat. No sooner did we get ashore and all hell broke loose at Holliwell Point. I've been living off the land, moving from one place to another and gradually heading for Canewdon. I thought I was going to be outdone at the finishing post when that lot went off last night. I've seen a few survivors here and there on my travels, but not stayed among them for too long. Large groups attract the machines, and I have more faith in my old skills to get me by."

"Yes, I would suppose a poacher could use such cunning skills to his advantage in the countryside. Especially evading the tripods," Llewellyn replied.

"Did you have trouble with dog packs? I was surprised how the strays quickly formed packs. For a time, I thought they would become very dangerous, but the machines were hunting and sucking their blood as much as they did humans. Especially the big formidable looking mutts."

"There were a few strays," Llewellyn answered. "I know the Martians went for people and sheep. I never saw them take any dogs, but what strays there were soon vanished."

The policeman and the poacher walked on along the patchwork, pink country lane.

"All this," Llewellyn waved his hand in a sweeping gesture. "It was originally an eerie landscape of parasitical bright red weed. Now it's diminishing to pink, and towards the natural green. Everything is encouraging. But now we have a fighting machine in our area. Still alive and heading towards a place where I know there are people."

They walked alongside the River Crouch as it flowed towards the sea. Lewis knew a small path that left the lane and hugged the hedgerows and woodlands. This route made things a little awkward for Llewellyn with his bicycle – so much so that he finally decided to abandon it in a small ditch. They came out upon a muddy shoreline where the river split in two. The River Roach ran a southerly course, with Foulness Island on the opposite bank. They headed south with the new river inlet and began to walk carefully along using the pink grassy embankments for cover in case the tripod might show up in the distance. The wind had suddenly picked up and the river had become a little choppy, all within a space of thirty minutes.

"It seems as though nature goes silent when the Martians appear. Now they're gone, the wind has come and the gulls are in the air."

"I know," replied Llewellyn looking up at the squawking birds. "It is strange, no doubt on that."

They continued cautiously for about twenty minutes, then came suddenly on an abandoned lifeboat upon the muddy shoreline and also heard a rifle bolt click from behind. The sound caused both men to freeze, and Gippy to start whining nervously.

"Shut up, Gippy!" Lewis growled as he turned with arms outstretched in surrender. A hare in each hand and his rifle still slung at his back out of harm's way. The little terrier complied instantly. Her tail went between its legs abjectly.

From the pink, wind-swept grassy dunes, foreign sailors emerged armed with rifles. They looked very nervous and dishevelled in their dirty, white uniforms.

"They're Froggies," said Llewellyn. "Do any of you speak English?"

"I do, sir," replied a middle-aged man with a thick French accent. He walked forward confidently and gave a command in French, at which the sailors lowered their rifles. There was a look of relief in each sailor's face, and it was apparent they were uneasy at being ashore.

"I take it you came ashore in the life boat earlier this morning," added Llewellyn.

"That is correct," replied the older Frenchman, and his huge friendly smile cut across his face. His bushy, black moustache and beard moved with his features. "I am what you English call a quartermaster. Quartermaster Blanc of F.S. *Ney* at your service, Constable." He held out a hand, which Llewellyn grasped firmly.

"I'm Police Constable Adrian Llewellyn. And I'm Welsh, not English, Mister Blanc," he laughed jovially. "Very pleased to meet you, very pleased indeed."

Lewis moved forward and shook the quartermaster's hand. "I'm Lewis Puttnam, very pleased to make your acquaintance, Sir."

"Likewise, Mister Puttnam, and thank you." He turned to his men, who were all politely coming forward with hands proffered to shake. "These are six crewmen from our ship. Most, I must sadly say, went down with our ship, but I hope others might have got ashore during the bombardment and under cover of night. We were at the rear of the convoy, and the other ships could not stop for us."

"And that is how you good gentlemen find yourselves here," added Llewellyn. "I'm sorry it could not have been in more congenial times, Mister Blanc."

The French sailors and the two Britons were beginning to warm to one another – as people do in times of great stress. Each was glad of the others' company. Each displayed courtesy and good intention.

"We are not sure where we are, Constable," said the French quartermaster, hoping that the policeman might be able to enlighten him. He held out his arm in the direction he wished them to go, beyond the dunes to a small hedgerow covered in dying pink weed.

Accepting the gesture, they walked over the grassy dunes towards the spot where a small fire was burning.

"No fires, sir!" Lewis was suddenly filled with panic, as was P.C. Llewellyn.

"My word, you don't want to be doing that now, lads." He looked to the quartermaster. "Fire attracts them like bees to a honey pot."

Quickly, the French quartermaster snapped out orders with a tone of urgency and his men extinguished the fire immediately.

Lewis was looking about the red-tinged landscape nervously, but there were no tripods anywhere. "It's definitely not like it was. Something might have appeared on the landscape just a few days ago, but now? I can't make out where they have all gone. We know there is one about and we think it may have gone to a village close by."

"They always seem to be heading in the direction of London when we do see them," added Llewellyn. He turned to Quartermaster Blanc and answered his original question. "You are in the County of Essex, Sir." As he regarded the sailors, it was obvious that the county meant nothing to them. "Well, the River Thames is a little way to the south," he pointed in the general direction. "It's not too far."

"Ah yes, I understand you. I was not sure how far north we had sailed when we got involved in the battle. There was a big convoy of ships. British, French, German and many other nations. We were able to fire a tremendous bombardment at them, but still they returned fire with their heat rays. They hit many of our ships, but we did hit at least two of them as the fleet steamed by."

"Have you heard much news of what is going on in other parts of the country?" asked Lewis.

The Frenchman smiled and nodded his head. "I know that your government is now operating from Edinburgh, and the Martians stopped on the outskirts of Glasgow."

"Really," replied Llewellyn, his interest suddenly keener.

Lewis interjected impatiently. "What made them stop before Glasgow?"

Again, Quartermaster Blanc smiled reassuringly. "They seem to be retreating. Why? We cannot say for sure, but we think they are ill. The British Army has pushed back down into northern England and found many of the machines abandoned. From Dublin, British Army Headquarters has landed an expeditionary force in Wales and they have found much the same. These messages have been coming from other ships and shoreline semaphore sites that are still operating up north. They have not been defeated by military might, they are ill. When we do come up against live ones, they are still as deadly as ever and don't hesitate to start firing heat rays and poisonous gas. But they always head south after the fighting. There are reports of the machines walking very sluggishly in huge lines over the Yorkshire dales and along the Pennines. Do you know of these places?"

"Yes," replied Llewellyn and Lewis in unison.

Lewis rubbed the back of his neck. "We have been thinking that we have not seen many of them lately until last night. Even the red weed is dying." He pointed beyond the grassy mounds by the shoreline where there was no red weed at all.

"Yes," agreed Quartermaster Blanc. "We have heard these reports too."

"There was the one that went towards Paglesham this morning. Mind, that one was injured, but it has not returned and there are still people in the village. It is our intention to go there and see if these people are all right," said Llewellyn.

"Perhaps my men and I could accompany you, Constable. There are seven of us in all and we might be able to give assistance," the quartermaster suggested with a polite smile.

"That would be greatly appreciated, Mister Blanc," replied P.C. Llewellyn sincerely. "Can we leave as soon as possible? I feel uneasy about the fire – if it does attract Martian attention, we need to be far away when they arrive."

"Of course," Quartermaster Blanc replied and turned to his men to bark more orders in French.

Each man gathered what few possessions he had and waited for the order to leave. They seemed eager to be away from the shoreline, and each sailor looked nervous. The epitome of men lost in a hostile and foreign land.

Quartermaster Blanc looked to the country policeman still neat in his uniform despite the tribulation of the land and smiled as though enjoying the eccentricity of the British. "So, Constable Llewellyn, we go to Pagle…" he stuttered trying to remember the pronunciation.

"Paglesham Mister Blanc, Paglesham Churchend, not Paglesham Eastend." He smiled humorously and looked to Lewis, who was still clutching his dead hares and his British Army issue rifle hanging behind his shoulder. "We'll let our famous village character lead the way. If you would be so kind, Lewis."

The old poacher chuckled and walked forward, adding to the constable "We would be best to approach by the Eastend village first. We can use the mud banks for cover and the hedgerows after leaving Eastend to cross the fields towards Churchend."

The sailors fell in line behind the old poacher, while Blanc and P.C. Llewellyn followed, covering the rear of the group. The British bobby and the French quartermaster enjoyed an exchange of information, which each was eager to offer in abundance.

About them, the green foliage of Mother Earth calmly nagged away at the red weed – gradually, but surely, claiming back patches of green. Lush dark green was beginning to spread, fresh growth recovering the dying, pink landscape.

CHAPTER 4

THE FIGHTING MACHINE AT PAGLESHAM CHURCHEND

Mrs Steed sat back in her chair, a special chair that she had for her special small table. From here, she liked to look out of the window and over the fields. Her end-of-terrace cottage was next to the church graveyard. The line of poplars to the front stopped just before her cottage – something she was grateful for. It allowed her a splendid view of the fields. Except that recently the lush green and the golden wheat of the English countryside had been invaded by the red weed. For a time, the alien parasite had got everywhere. Most of the summer, in fact. But now, the red weed was dying. *Praise be to God.* The vibrant green was winning back, reclaiming the land.

The machines had not been seen either. At least, not up close. There had been an offshore engagement the previous night, but that was on the other side of the River Crouch, by Holliwell Point. The Martians and their machines were apparently elsewhere. They had lost interest in the remote area of Paglesham Churchend. This had been the case for a couple of weeks. The last testing time had been back when the army unit had been attacked at Paglesham Eastend. Then the dreadful plundering of her village again, after the army unit had been destroyed.

Mrs Steed clasped her locket on her chest. Inside was a photo of Anne, her late daughter. She thought of her grandson, Jimmy, a precious gift from her deceased daughter. Then she reached across the table for the photo stand. It displayed the same, but larger, portrait of Anne. How she missed her.

She whispered to the photograph. "I've been trying my best, Anne. There have been such terrible events for us to confront. I don't mean Reggie and his condition. He has been doing very well. He has been a godsend in the terrible circumstances we have had to endure. It is almost like Reggie was made for this world. A world of creatures from outer space. Horrible things from Mars. Jimmy and Reggie have been with me all of the time. I think many thousands of people have been killed. Many hundreds of thousands. Perhaps millions!

The Last Days of the Fighting Machine

"We have managed to hide from these monsters in their giant machines. We have done very well to keep out of their way. There does not seem too many of them now. P.C. Llewellyn from Canewdon insists the Martians are dying. Because of this news, we have been venturing out.

"Jimmy went out without permission this morning. He kept asking if he could go across the meadow to Eastend. That is because he felt sure the unit of soldiers that were killed some weeks back would have army issue food rations. He said they might have tinned food, which would not go off. If he could find such things among the corpses of the soldiers, we might have a little more food.

"Of course, I forbade him to go. I forbade Reg as well. Yet I knew your Jimmy might be correct about the tinned food. I wanted to wait a day or two longer. Then I wanted us all to go together. However, Jimmy took it upon himself to sneak out early this morning without permission. I was so angry, and was about to go after him. Reggie got agitated and began to panic. He was worried about Jimmy but was also worried about me leaving the cottage. In the end, I agreed to let Reggie go out and find him. Now I'm waiting for them to come back. I'm sure they will get back soon. I'm just so very anxious, waiting for them."

A tear came to Mrs Steed's eye as she looked at the photo of her much loved daughter. "They will be back soon. I'm sure of it. I love you, Anne, and we will meet each other again. Somewhere else. Anywhere but here."

Mrs Steed put the photo back and jumped upright out of her seat. Total alarm and dread shook her person.

Alaghhh!

The cry of the fighting machine. That hideous sound was unmistakable. The things were still about. The dreadful monster could not be one of the two from the previous night. She and her boys believed they had seen the fighting machines devoured by explosion and flame from the battleships. This must be another fighting one, or perhaps one was injured and is now coming to Paglesham Churchend?

Mrs Steed quickly made for the front door. She opened it and walked into the open village road, out towards the line of poplar trees. She could hear the thud and crash of the huge machine growing louder. Then its vile body appeared above the woodlands before the village.

"Oh, my God!" she screamed. The tripod was coming towards Paglesham Churchend. Its battle cry was ringing out over the village. For some reason, she assumed the first alien cry was for Reggie and Jimmy at Paglesham Eastend. The machine would be able to see any movement across the open meadow. Even the patchy pink and green would

The Last Days of the Fighting Machine

expose her two boys. She was wrong. It was not so. The machine was coming towards her. Had she been spotted? Mrs Steed swallowed in fear. Her heart was thumping as she started to back slowly away. The giant mechanism waded into the woodland. She could hear the branches cracking and falling as the Martian machine came directly towards her. Then she turned and made back for her front door.

Argh-laaaa!

The machine bellowed amid the cacophony of breaking branches. It sent her blood cold. She stumbled through her front door, slamming it behind her. There was the crash of the giant's step. One huge leg must have been out of the woods and upon the dry mud track of the village road. My God, how fast the thing could move. Another loud crash shook the very ground, and she stumbled against the wall. The Martian had to be outside. Probably looking down at the cottages. The front window smashed. A crescendo of broken glass and splintering wood. Her desk and her daughter's photo were among the flying debris of shattered things.

Instinct kicked in. Not up the stairs. Its many arms would be crashing through the windows upstairs. Her instinct was to go to ground. She made for the door by the staircase but the huge machine appendage that had smashed the front window came through the door. Mrs Steed froze. The machine's feeler twisted and turned to her. There was a lens upon its end. It was staring at her. The thing was humming. A strange sound, like a gathering of agitated bees, but she knew it to be some inner mechanised working.

She went against her instincts and ran up the stairs. The door beneath the staircase was blocked now. The humming of the appendage seemed to grow louder – as though she had excited it. Mrs Steed nimbly reached the top landing. The machine's twisting feeler was pursuing her. It followed her up the stairs.

More crashing of glass as one of the upstairs bedroom windows were destroyed. Another appendage from the machine. It knew she was there, and it was determined to have her. Mrs Steed tried to contain herself but the panic within was taking over. She had witnessed the bloodsucking of her neighbour, Mrs Walker, when a fighting machine had taken her. That awful moment, when the barbed syringes went into the wretched women and she was pumped with a vile substance that had caused her to convulse as though she was having a fit. Jimmy had fits.

Oh God, what of poor Jimmy and Reg? Who would look after her boys?

Mrs Steed trembled as the vision of Mrs Walker's final moments came back to her tortured recollection. The poor woman was sucked dry of her blood by the second barbed syringe. The first to insert something into her body and the second to drain it dry. Oh, how hideous it all was for Mrs Walker. How hideous it was going to be for Mrs Steed.

She screamed as an appendage shot out of the bedroom along the landing and entwined its feeler about her waist. Violently, she was pulled towards the bedroom doorway, hitting her head against the door jamb with enough force to split the skin along her hair line. Again she screamed, as blood cascaded down the side of her face. In panic, she was kicking and thrashing, lifted off of the floor. It was all too much. The room was twisting about while she was gripped about by the mechanical tendril. She vaguely remembered the smashed bedroom window coming towards her, the pain in her arm as a glass shard sliced through the white sleeve of her blouse sleeve.

Suddenly, Mrs Steed was outside, held high in the air, suspended above the roof of her cottage. Her long leather brown boots were dangling, with no firm footing below. The breeze was swirling tattered strands of long hair free from her updo. Sticky blood was congealing on her head. The intensified terror and vertigo made her heart pound. She struggled to gather her thrashed and petrified wits. Something hideous was inside of the machine's trunk. She could see a distorted silhouette of the alien through the murky green port hole. She squinted through her tears. Her vision was as hazy as the jade opening of the machine's body trunk. The dizzy height, the breeze, the horrifying scrutiny and then the blackness overtook her. She fainted. Shock and horror caused the darkness to jerk forward. It was welcome. The terror was gone. For the moment.

A gentle breeze swept across patchy clumps of pallid pink foliage. There were also expanding clumps of vibrant green grass, which seemed to be overwhelming the sickly red weed. The alien undergrowth had once been a vibrant and rich red colour. It had till recently surrounded the small village of Paglesham Churchend. Now it was dying. Mother Earth was fighting back. Everywhere, the red weed was in decline. As the once abundant red faded to a sickly pink, the alien vegetation seemed to decay and blow away. There were dusty flakes in the mild and indifferent breeze.

There was the Earthly promise of autumn, which lent hope that the Martian vegetation was dying. Hugging the hedgerows were two people. A young boy of eleven and a tall man of about thirty. Cautiously, they had been creeping along the hedge, using trees and ditches to obscure their approach. Upon reaching a particular deep part of the hedgerow's parallel ditch, they stopped to take stock of their situation.

The young boy surveyed their surroundings, wiping his sweaty hands nervously upon his creased and dirty white shirt. It was evident that both had suffered traumatic experiences.

"We're almost there, Uncle Reg. If it's still there, we should see it when we get around the trees up ahead." He began to shake, feeling that his responsibilities were getting too much for him.

His uncle reached out a huge hand, gently resting it upon the youngster's shoulder to reassure him. "Don't worry, Jimmy. We'll find my mum and she'll know what to do." His unconfident words were slow and laboured, like those of a child. It was no more than to be expected from Reg.

Young Jimmy smiled at his uncle and nodded. How pleased he was of his Uncle Reg's presence. The formidable man may have had a mental handicap, but he was as strong as a bull. This was a source of security in such harsh and terrifying times. He remembered his late mother getting very angry when people referred to her brother as mongoloid. Jimmy hated the name, too. He was told that the term meant something similar to Mongol people, who once had a great empire. How people with his Uncle Reg's condition were called mongoloid after an Asiatic people was beyond him. It upset his grandmother too. He recalled her getting cross with the local doctor who had referred to Uncle Reg as Mongoloid.

"We will find Granny, Reg. She is probably worried that the fighting machine has got us. You know how Granny worries about us."

Reg gently squeezed his nephew's shoulder. "We will find mum. We must be careful. That machine must be beyond the trees and still in the village. The last time they came, they stood by the church tower. They stood next to it to hide. I think that is why they stand by tall things. It is the only way they can hide."

Jimmy looked out again across the blustery meadow. He frowned while scrutinising the hedgerow. "Yes, Uncle Reg. I think you are right. It will be standing by the belfry. Just like the others did."

"What are you looking at, Jimmy?" The uncertainty in the slow, deep voice betrayed his poor uncle's disability, yet his sense of devotion to his nephew was never in doubt.

"The red weed on the hedge is turning a sickly looking pink. And out in the meadows too. The grass patches are becoming green again. It is happening all over the place. The red weed is dying and our green is coming back." There was a tone of

The Last Days of the Fighting Machine

greater excitement in Jimmy's voice. "Just as things were looking good, one of those machines comes back – blast the thing!"

Reg reached forward and broke off a stem of the red weed and crushed it between his fingers and thumb, rubbing it into dust.

"It's breaking like ice," said Jimmy. "Do you think it could be dying, Uncle Reg?" There was a nervous glimmer of hope inside of him. He fretfully scratched his leg through baggy and dishevelled grey flannels.

"Could be," replied Reg as he looked down at the crushed weed in his huge palm. His big jaw dropped and his chin moved right then left before settling back beneath his top teeth. His huge puckered lips protruded as though about to dribble, though he never did. "It might be because autumn is coming." He looked at Jimmy with uneven ears that stuck out the side of his head in a most unflattering spectacle. "Perhaps red weed dies too early for autumn?" He brushed the alien plant dust away and, like Jimmy, wiped his hands on his dirty, white, baggy shirt and grey trousers.

Jimmy's optimism died instantly. "Oh yes. I did not think of that." He then stopped and looked up into the sky. The wind swept back his light brown hair. "Hold on, Uncle. It's still late summer and the last day of August. Would plants from another planet grow by our seasons? I've learnt about this sort of thing at school during physical geography. A plant from foreign countries has changes during different times to us in Britain, so something from Mars would have to be stranger still."

Reg just stared, a little bemused by what his nephew had just said, knowing that the youngster had always excelled at school. "Plants do what weather tells them," he added, what he thought to be true. He frowned and looked at the sickly pink of the red weed's stems as the parasite tried to feebly cling to the strong green stems and leaves. "It is a blustery day, but not cold." He looked up at the clear, blue sky and his nostrils flared as he took in the country air. "The red weed sent is not in the air either."

Jimmy began to sniff and his face brightened with hope. "Yes, you are right, Uncle. It must be dying, and it's dying in the summer. It's not autumn yet." His breathing became excited as he began to look around, enthusiastically searching for further signs. "You said that the fighting machine was moving strangely when it went to Churchend. Maybe it was dying too. It's been the only one to visit in almost two weeks and, apart from last night, there are no distant guns or ray fire on the horizon. There was always glowing, but that has all gone over the past week or so. There has been nothing except that

The Last Days of the Fighting Machine

sluggish tripod this morning. It walked like it was drunk. It disappeared behind the trees. We know it has gone into Churchend and it has not come back out. Not even called. Maybe the Martian things are ill? Perhaps it is standing by the belfry again because it needs to hide. This area is very remote."

"Everywhere is re, re... empty. Nowhere is crowded anymore. The people have run away. Be careful, Jimmy, you are getting excited again. My mum said to watch for you getting excited."

"Nanny thinks I might have a fit, but I have not had one since I was nine." He calmed down and went silent for a moment and looked fearfully at the trees. "We are in a difficult situation. I know Nanny is going to be very cross with me, but I knew there might be food in the soldiers' kit bags at Paglesham Eastend. That's why I tried to creep across the fields. I just wanted it to be all right and thought it would take a couple of hours if I kept to the ditches and hedgerows."

"You should not have gone, Jimmy. Mum was very cross and worried, and now Mum will be cross with the both of us since I had to come and find you. And now there is a fighting machine in Churchend."

Jimmy sighed miserably. "I could not even search the deserted homes. It was the sight of all the dead soldiers by the small bridge. The ones that had come up from Foulness." He began to reminisce morbidly. "Some must have tried to flee to Eastend village. The smell was awful. They've been lying about for weeks. Some of the dead soldiers were inside the cottages covered in the black soot. The Martians must have smothered the area with that poisonous smoke. It killed them all where they were hiding. Other bodies were in the lane. The soldiers had fled from the cottages, choking and twisting. Dying as they wriggled for breath. I would have been back with you within hours. I didn't know this new machine would come. Nothing has come in weeks. Nanny must be beside herself with worry."

"Mum told us, 'always go to ground, even if it is days before a tripod moves on.' Mum will know we are doing that." Reg looked to the trees anxiously, then turned back to Jimmy and began to doubt what they were doing. "She will be cross that we are doing this when there is a machine monster in the village."

"We don't know if it is there for sure, Uncle. It probably is. The trees do hide Churchend from view. We are low down. Therefore, we look upwards over the trees. Even something as big as a fighting machine is out of view. We have not seen it leave. It could have gone north into the river. We would not have seen that."

"I would have heard it, Jimmy. It is still there, but it is quiet now. It has stopped making a noise, and that is strange. They usually scream out when they are doing things, but this one has stopped. Has it stopped doing things? Why has it stopped? Has it done what it wanted in Churchend?"

Jimmy bit his lip. "Everything has gone quiet, and I think we might need to find Nanny now." His face was etched with concern. "We need to know Nanny is all right, and Nanny will want to know of us. Besides, Nanny might be in trouble, Uncle Reg. Maybe the fighting machine is waiting the way the others did when they first came to the village and took the Walkers in that cage thing at the back of them. When Nanny took us away from the village and out into the hedgerow ditches to wait until the Martian machines had gone. It might even use the black smoke, the way it did with the soldiers."

Reg frowned, nervous at the thought. He scratched his unkempt brown hair, then rubbing the stubble upon his jaw where three days of growth made him feel decidedly untidy. "We should have left with the others," he muttered in his childlike manner.

"I think Nanny was right to make us stay. Thousands of people would attract the machines. They suck the blood out of people they capture. It happened to the Walkers. I bet the machine monsters attacked the big crowds of people as they all left. I think thousands must have died. We are far away here. Southend and Rochford are the closest towns and we know what happed there. That's why the sky was glowing red for days and nights."

"Do you think that Queen Victoria got away?" asked Uncle Reg naively.

"I would hope so, Uncle. I would hate the Queen to go through what poor Mrs Walker did." He began to tremble with fear as he thought back to the scene. They were forced to watch from the hedgerows. The village publicans, Mister and Mrs Walker, had been taken by the Martians. He shuddered at the memory. Mrs Walker had screamed and wriggled while flexible tubes with thorns punctured her helpless body and drained her of blood. The convulsive fits and vomiting as the wretched lady had hung there in mid-air. Her life being sucked from her. Poor Mister Walker had screamed helplessly from the cage at the back of the fighting machine, pathetically wailing as the tripod machine walked off with him into the night, having devoured the poor man's wife before his very eyes.

Reg put an arm around his frightened nephew. He sensed Jimmy was reliving that horror. That dreadful night back in July. "It was many weeks back, Jimmy. Mummy says, 'Things have gone quiet.' Except for that last strange one that came today and the guns last night. I really don't think the machine thing is well. There is something wrong with it." He

The Last Days of the Fighting Machine

felt young Jimmy shaking at the thought. "Please try and put poor Mrs Walker out of your mind, Jimmy. She is in heaven now. Maybe all the tripods are ill. Like the red weed."

Jimmy sat bolt upright and, again, scrutinised the pinking colour of the Martian weed. "You might be right," he muttered with renewed hope. "Things do seem to be changing."

Reg smiled at him with his usual boyish grin and young eyes. "Let's creep along towards the trees."

"Yes," agreed Jimmy. "We must approach Churchend under cover of the woods."

Carefully they continued along the ditch, following the hedgerow as it arced along the dried mud lane towards the woodland. The copse obscured their view of Paglesham Churchend. All the time, Reg and Jimmy were vigilant in case the giant machine should suddenly appear. The trees were big enough to obscure one and with this firmly in mind their courage and resolve needed constant massaging.

"We must find Nanny," whispered Jimmy. "That's all that matters."

Reg nodded his approval, then raised a finger to his lips for silence. He pointed to the tree foliage and mimed the words. "No red weed!"

Jimmy was surprised to realise that there was barely any of the Martian weed at all in the trees.

Just an odd section of fading pink in remote areas here and there.

"It must be dying; there can be no other reason."

"Be careful, Jimmy, it could be in the trees."

"It would be above the trees," added Jimmy. "The tripods are taller than the trees."

"They can crouch like people and hide in woods. We've seen them squat when they were searching inside the houses with their wire arm things."

"Tentacles. Nanny called them tentacles. Octopuses have them."

"What are octopuses?" Reg was bewildered, and found some of his nephew's knowledge a little intimidating at times.

Upon reaching the woods they carefully climbed out of the ditch and crawled into the trees. Each got behind a tree trunk and very carefully stood up. Jimmy looked to his Uncle Reg. "Are we going through the woods?"

"Yes, there is a lot of cover here." He peered around the tree deeper into the dark woodlands. "It's all clear, follow me and stop when I do, Jimmy."

"I will, Uncle," he replied and immediately fell behind Reg as they stealthily made their way into the wood. Finally reaching a big oak, they stopped to survey the next part of the journey. It would bring them to the fringe of the woods that looked out upon Paglesham Churchend. The all-clear was agreed by both and they made a final dash through the trees to the woods' end. The mud road was before them and on the other side the almost deserted village. Not that Paglesham Churchend had ever been a bustling place. All the buildings were in line. A public house, a line of cottages and then a bolder-wall perimeter; beyond was a small graveyard mound, upon which stood Paglesham church. Before the buildings on the other side of the muddy road was a row of tall poplar trees. Horses and carts would come into Paglesham before the cottages and leave by the back of the poplar trees, turning by the church at the end of the village. Beyond was a further tall hedge wall with one small opening. There was a stile for people to climb over. Beyond was a path that led down to a boatyard running part way along the mud banks.

"I still can't see the machine," whispered Reg, concerned. "Even the red weed creepers here are going pink. Look at the pub wall."

"It's changing everywhere." Jimmy's heart skipped a beat and he began to feel very uneasy about not knowing where the machine could be. "How can it not be seen? It's a giant machine monster. It can't hide."

"Calm down, Jimmy." Reg was beginning to worry about him.

Jimmy breathed a sigh, knowing why Reg needed reassurance. "I won't have a fit, Uncle. Honest. I haven't had one for over two years."

"We must go around the back of the houses, along the backyard walls. It might be in the church yard. We can't see that from here. The cottages are hiding the belfry. They can hide a fighting machine too."

"All right, let's go." He sped off across the mud lane and made his way towards the public house, with Reg jogging close behind.

Reaching the wall of the derelict public house, they pressed themselves against the dying red weed and paused briefly, before figuring their next move. There was an overturned horse cart and shattered glass all along the lane where the deserted cottages stood.

"Much of this debris is from weeks back when the first machines came. I can't see any new wreckage." There was a glimmer of hope in Jimmy's voice.

"Only Mum would be here. There would be no others." Reg was uneasy and wanted desperately to get home to their cottage, which was at the end of the terrace, next to the church wall. "We'll go around the back," he repeated as he unlatched the side door that led into the back yard of the public house.

Carefully they tiptoed across the yard, scaled a small wall and dropped into the adjoining back garden to the cottage next door. Again, they listened and surveyed their immediate surroundings before going to the back door, which led to the rear walkway behind the terraces.

"We're almost there, Uncle," whispered Jimmy.

He was answered by Reg's forefinger that was firmly pressed to his lip. "Shush now, Jimmy," he hissed quietly.

Furtively they crept along the back-alley, crouching behind the line of pink and green bushes. These offered some shelter to anything that might be observing from the open meadow behind the cottages. Quickly, they got to the end of the alley and entered their own backyard. Reg suddenly froze and held out an arm, stopping young Jimmy dead in his tracks. Instinctively, they moved sideways and hid behind the garden shed.

"What is wrong, Uncle?" Panic gripped Jimmy and he asked again. "What has happened?"

"It's the roof. There's a big hole and all the roof slates are gone."

Jimmy leaned forward and saw the damage for himself as his vision combed upwards along the clinging red creepers. It stopped at the gaping cavity and broken roof tiles. It was new and could only have been done by the latest machine to visit the village.

"It has been searching about with them tentacle things," Jimmy said tensely. "Good God! Nanny! Is Nanny all right?" He ran foreword, with Reg hotly in pursuit. They burst through the scullery door. Both were gripped with absolute dread and panic.

Jimmy was beside himself. Not his grandmother, not now. "Oh my God, Nanny…"

Reg's hand clasped his mouth. "Calm down, Jimmy, and don't shout." He was trying to soothe the youngster, while trying to contain his own child-like emotions. He knew he was not as able as other adults, but he had to do his best by Jimmy. His late sister's son might be all that he had left in a world where nature had been cruel to him. Long before the world had changed and dealt cruelty out upon a scale never envisaged by anyone. "Shout and it might hear. We will search for my mum now, and quietly. Understand, Jimmy?"

Gently, Reg released his hand. His look conveyed the genuine concern he felt for Jimmy. "We must be quiet," he whispered. "I think the machine monster is close. Maybe in the graveyard. That is why we did not see it."

"How do you know that?" Jimmy was shaking and sweating with fear. Somehow, he knew his uncle was right. The church, and its grounds, was the only area they had not been able to inspect. The tripod fighting machines were huge. Hardly things that went unnoticed.

"First let us look for my Mummy." He sighed, and his body language told of someone void of hope. "Every room and under the stairs then the attic."

The Last Days of the Fighting Machine

Demoralised, Reg and Jimmy went about the task of searching. As they turned over the wrecked furniture in each room, it was ever more depressing to realise she was gone. There had been an obvious struggle. Overturned beds, wardrobe and broken vases. In the back bedroom there was a huge hole where the ceiling plaster had been smashed in and there were signs of a struggle. A trail of blood ran along the floor, up the wall and on down the smashed and broken window.

"The tentacles from the tripod have been searching in here. They must have caught Nanny," wept Jimmy. "Oh God, poor Nanny and we were not there to help."

A suppressed snivel came from Reg as he gritted his teeth and fell to his knees clasping his hands to his chest. Stricken with grief, his body shook. Had the inevitable dug deep into him?

"Mummy," he whimpered softly, while within a burning hate-fed rage festered. Again he whimpered: "Mummy," slowly shaking his head in disbelief.

Jimmy felt helpless as he watched the grown man shake like a little child because his mother had been taken from him. He had a mental age of Jimmy's level, but there was a will within him and he had been taught a strong sense of inner control. Slowly, Reg allowed his sobbing to abate, while his nephew looked on helpless. As the moments passed, the mentally challenged man stood up. He took a deep breath and looked to Jimmy with tear-drenched cheeks. He gulped and held out his arms for his nephew. Jimmy moved forward for the embrace.

Jimmy started to sob, while his simple Uncle Reg consoled him as best he could.

"We must try and find Nanny. She can't be far and she must be buried properly."

Reg nodded his head in agreement. "We will, Jimmy, and I bet that bastard machine monster is in the churchyard. I think Mummy will be close by. I'm going into the attic to look into the church grounds. There we can look and stay hidden."

There were no side-windows in the end-of-terrace cottage, so there was no view towards the churchyard.

"I'm coming too, Uncle, I'm not staying on my own. If we go, it will be together."

His uncle gripped him on the shoulder firmly and added. "We stick together for always, Jimmy. Come on, let's see what is in the churchyard."

Together, they carefully left the bedroom and moved out to the landing where the trap door to the loft was."

"The bastard thing dragged Mum through the bedroom window," said Reg.

Gingerly, he reached up and lifted the trap door and was able to move it along the loft rafters. Instead of the usual darkness, shafts of daylight came from the roof's hole, where the tripod had smashed its tentacle arm through the slates.

"I'll go up first and reach down for you." Reg put a foot upon the banister rail and lifted himself up into the hatchway. He then reached down for Jimmy and hauled him up with comparative ease.

Jimmy was about to stand but felt his uncle's hand upon his shoulder, gently restraining him. "Be careful, Jimmy, and copy me," he whispered and then slowly stood. "Put your feet on the rafters, Jimmy." He moved over to the corner of the attic using the daylight from the roof's hole to guide him. His nephew followed, copying his moves.

Some of the slates had been dislodged and had slipped to allow use as peep holes.

"We must stay well clear of that big hole. Spy out of the small openings," whispered Jimmy, as they peered out over the graveyard to the old church.

Jimmy caught his breath. The immobile, monstrous machine filled his vision. Sweat started to ooze from every pore of his body. His heart began to pound inside his chest. He felt faint and gripped the roof-joist to steady himself. He battled the fear that had brought about spasmodic shaking. Gritting his teeth, he willed himself to look again and drank in the sight. The colossal machine was standing motionless next to the tall church spire where green ivy was battling with the dying red weed for dominance over the stone blocked structure. The grotesque alien stood guard over the defeated relic of man's faith. Its huge legs stood to the height of the church spire, where joints like elbows or knees had further limb extensions hanging down, cradling the dirty light grey body trunk between the lower limbs. It resembled an enormous gnat. When it stood, the body trunk would rise as the limb extensions rose above the lower joints, giving the fighting machine even greater height. There was the usual small, green porthole to the front of the body trunk.

"It's just standing there," whispered Reg with awe.

"I can't see Nanny," stuttered Jimmy as he surveyed the surrounding graves that were clustered with the creeping pale red weed.

"The machine's body is close to the upper window where the bell is," said Reg.

Jimmy followed his Uncle's line of vision and noted a small platform leading from the machine's body to the window of the belfry. "The Martians must have come out and gone into the spire through that window. Why would they do that?"

"They must be looking for something," replied Reg in his slow bewildered tone.

"Maybe Nanny is in there." He began to feel angry and revolted that the atrocious Martians would take his grandmother. How he craved the opportunity to inflict some momentous hurt upon the obscene anonymity of the alien creatures. He looked at the small, green, opaque bulge to the front of the machine. The strange porthole protruded from the dull alloy, like some compound membrane. A vile mucus that almost made him retch. The misty aperture was like the eye of a giant insect. The sight filled him with disgust.

"That thing has been hit by cannon or something," added Reg innocently.

Jimmy's attention was captured instantly as he looked to his uncle. "Where...? What do you mean, cannon fire?"

"You might not be able to see from your side. Come here," Reg whispered.

The youngster carefully made his way to his uncle's location and peeped through the hole before him. "Oh God! You are right, Uncle Reg. That thing has been hit by a shell. There is a black, scorched hole to the side of it. I wonder how that happened."

"It looks like dry blood down the side of the machine, but machines don't bleed." Reg was all the more confused.

"We must get into the church, Uncle. Nanny is in there and if the Martians are not in the machine, they can be hurt." Jimmy had become uncomfortably bold with his simmering anger.

"No, Jimmy," stuttered his uncle. "Mum would go mad at me if I let you go in there."

"Uncle, those things killed Nanny and I want one. Nanny is in there, and I bet that's where they drank her blood." He was becoming hysterical with frustration and rage. "We can't leave her in there."

Reg sighed, but was also compelled by an overwhelming desire to do something. Like all young boys, he was easily led by notions of anger and revenge. The terrible danger that was before them and their foolish venture was clouded by a fog of adrenalin and fuelled by fury.

"I'm going to the pub."

"Why?" Jimmy was confused.

"Mister Walker had a gun. I used to go poaching with him and Lewis Puttnam. He let me use it. He kept it in his pub. It must be still there."

"You can get a shotgun?" asked Jimmy in awe.

"Yes, I think so, and then we must creep past the front wall of the church and enter at the entrance where the machine thing can't see us." He began to breathe heavily with excitement and fear, but still there was resolve that ran through both of their immature minds. "We can get in there, Jimmy. We can do it."

"Let's go to Mister Walker's place, then."

Jimmy began to move towards the trap door while Reg took one more peep at the tripod through

The Last Days of the Fighting Machine

the loose slating. The view only offered a vision of the front of the machine but the cage, which he knew was on top of the machine's body, could not be seen. Sometimes the Martians kept people inside the enclosures before blood sucking. He reflected upon the final ordeal of poor Mr Walker who was kept in the cage, probably for some time – screaming and lamenting for his wife, whom he had seen fiendishly killed. Mr Walker had been left and carried away to await the same fate sometime later.

"Come on, Uncle Reg," hissed Jimmy.

Reg complied, stealthily moving to the trap door and lowering Jimmy onto the landing. "We will do this, Jimmy, but we must be quite and very careful."

"We will, Uncle," he whispered back. "We will."

CHAPTER 5

THE MUD BANKS OF WALLASEA ISLAND

Lewis stopped abruptly and held up his hand, signalling for the rest to come to a halt. There were gasps of amazement and horror from the French sailors when they saw the carnage of fat-bloated and rotting corpses upon the mud banks. Swarms of flies buzzed in the putrid air and crows squawked amid the carnage, pecking around the dead.

"Oh, Mon Dieu!" muttered Lefebvre. He held his arm across his face, a vain attempt to block the smell of putrefaction.

"They're soldiers," said Lewis turning to P.C. Llewellyn who came forward with the French quartermaster. "God, the smell is awful." He put a handkerchief to his mouth and just refrained from gagging. Some of the French sailors did the same.

Lewis forced himself to look. He had seen such sights before, and on a grander scale. He remembered such things at Maldon and shuddered at the flashback of women and children screaming before the unfeeling tripods. The alien machines had been spitting heat and poisonous black smoke upon everyone. Finally, he turned, and Llewellyn gripped his arm.

"Are you all right, Lewis?"

"Yeah, I'm all right, thanks." There were tears in his eyes, but the will to go on also burned. He had become hardened. He told himself that too much self-indulgence was of no use. The dead were gone, the living had to fight on. Beside him, little Gippy growled her disapproval. But she refrained from barking, while her nose wrinkled before the dreadful stench.

"There is not much we can do for these poor souls," said Blanc with calm reasoning. "We must move on."

Lewis met the old French quartermaster's considerate gaze. "We need to scavenge, Mister Blanc. They are soldiers who were caught in the open and therefore died where they stood." He pointed to the dead on the mud banks. "They've been washed down, but I think there were more, further down where the River Roach bends towards Paglesham Eastend. I think they were hit by a small bridge.

There was a semaphore unit stationed on Foulness, and these men were something to do with that. I can remember these soldiers being stationed just before I left for Maldon in the early days of the meteors."

"That's right, and they put up a makeshift bridge to Foulness from this side of the island." Llewellyn also remembered the activity in the early days. "The Martians were out this way for some time, and caused great disorder."

Blanc listened and then looked across the muddy tributary to Foulness. He was slightly amused by the British notion of Foulness being an island; one could easily walk across to the place when the tide was out, as it was on this occasion.

"What do you mean by scavenge, Mister Lewis?"

"It's just Lewis," he smiled. "If these soldiers were hit upstream near the bridge and some were killed on dry land, then we might find some weaponry intact. We could use that." He nodded towards Blanc's men and added. "Not all of your men are armed and I think it would be best if we all had weapons, Sir."

Blanc smiled and nodded his approval. "You are correct, Lewis, it would be a wise thing to make for this bridge in the hope of such a find." He looked back at the decomposing corpses and his smile vanished. "I don't suppose this is going to be a very pleasant task."

"That's putting it very mildly, Mister Blanc – very mildly indeed," observed Llewellyn.

They pressed on, passing around the corpses up onto the pink-patched grassy rise, which caused Lewis to be more alert. He preferred hugging the dips and ditches in the land. It had become second nature and the open, bleak rises in the marshland left him feeling vulnerable to the fighting machines that could spot them over vast distances. He wondered if they were becoming careless because of the dwindling activity of the Martians.

"Are you all right, Lewis?" asked the quartermaster.

"Yes, Mister Blanc, but we should get down on the mud banks once we are past the dead soldiers. It is always best to keep to the low ground."

Blanc, frowning, looked about the exposed expanse and realised that the poacher made sense. "Yes, I agree with you."

He turned to his men and gave instructions that they would comply with the poacher's advice as soon as they were past the stench of the rotting corpses.

Their pace quickened as all became aware of the danger. Once beyond the dead, they immediately went back down onto the mud banks. They felt more settled in the seclusion of the lower ground.

Lewis felt compelled to elaborate more as to why they were keeping to the mud banks. "If we had cut across the island, we would be at Paglesham by now, Mister Blanc, but it would be over open land."

"I understand your reasoning well, Lewis, and appreciate that you have survived over the months when many have perished. I am open to anything you might say concerning guidance across this deranged and dangerous landscape." He turned to P.C. Llewellyn. "Lewis I can understand. He has managed to evade capture through his cunning ability as a poacher. You on the other hand are an enigma, sir. How did you come through all this intact and clean? You look as though life as gone on as normal and that Martians had never come to Earth."

"Well," began Llewellyn. "I laid low, like a lot of folk. We did not all run for the ports. I felt uneasy about being involved in the mass exodus and all. You see, I had to have orders. There were none. Communication was cut off. I had to make my own decisions. I thought of looters, too. Outsiders coming to the deserted village of Canewdon. In the end, I was looting the houses in search of food. I decided to let myself off with a stern warning. I stayed put and decided not to go with the refugees. Multitudes of people seemed to attract Martians and, quite honestly, I did not really know what to do. I just stayed at the station and never moved. I saw the fighting machines come and go. I had my own hiding place in

The Last Days of the Fighting Machine

Canewdon, which I used whenever they were about. The village was deserted and the Martians seemed to pay less attention after a while. I could even go out on my bicycle. That's how I discovered Mrs Steed and her family at Paglesham. I rode into the village one day and the simple chap, Reg, came out to greet me. Things did seem to go quiet. Of course, I heard all of the far-off terror and saw the night sky lighting up. Heard the explosions, and even saw some people from a distance being captured by the machines and tossed into the cages fixed to the back of these giant contraptions. But I managed to stay clear of the Martians in their fighting machines. There was the sound of the offshore battle last night, but apart from that, nothing close for some time.

"Today, I saw the first Martian fighting machine up close for well over two weeks. It was sick and injured. I know we only see the machine and the creatures are inside, but this thing was trailing smoke and it strode along as though it was broken. Almost like it was limping. I don't know why, but it went towards Paglesham Churchend. That is where Mrs Steed, her backward son Reg and her grandson Jimmy are. She always said go to ground until they are gone and I am assuming that she has. But I can't help worrying about her and her kin.

"Now, with last night's offshore fight between the Navy and the fighting machines, the terror of the Martians is back. Especially with this crippled thing coming this morning. Suddenly the blasted things have returned. The small bit of seclusion that began to make us feel a little secure has gone."

Lewis and P.C. Llewellyn walked along the mud with Blanc, while the other six French sailors chatted among themselves in their own language. They all walked slowly and cautiously as though none really wanted to get to the place they were heading for.

"I have been up north to Scotland. It is true that there are many up north who think the Martians are ill." Blanc scratched his sideburns. "They say the fighting machines are not as intense as they used to be. That battle we had last night was one of the most concentrated encounters we have seen in weeks. We lost our ship, yet we were able to defeat them. They had no reinforcements to come to their aid and, of the two fighting machines, one was lost and the other is injured. Everyone that I come across firmly believes that there is something wrong with them. They are returning southwards and dying along the way."

"I can agree with that. I've seen many forsaken machines in the fields," said Lewis. "They're dead. Just standing there like rotting monuments."

"I also hope you are right, Mister Blanc," replied Llewellyn with a reassuring smile. "But the things are still dangerous and formidable when they do show. I don't think we can count our chickens yet."

Blanc smiled. "Count your chickens? Another charming English expression, no doubt?"

Llewellyn laughed. "Perhaps we might live to enjoy such things if we are cautious. If these Martians are ill, they might yet perish altogether. I wonder what could make them ill so suddenly."

Perhaps it was something the bastards ate," replied Lewis. "They don't seem fussy about what they suck up."

Llewellyn raised a disapproving eyebrow. "Yes, thank you for that Lewis."

Blanc smiled. "When you are at sea you see a lot of things. You travel to many places and come across diseases. Sometimes local people seem oblivious, while European seafarers can catch all manner of things. Also, I've heard of a common cold causing loss of life among remote islands where its people have never come across such things. They would catch them from us. We seafarers would not always be able to help them. There must be many things that would not bother us but be deadly to an alien that had never come up against them. Something like a common cold, and if they suck blood, as I have heard, what sort of things might the Martians pick up that would be deadly to them?"

"Everything going, I hope," replied Lewis indulging himself at the thought. He looked at Blanc with a wicked and humorous glint in his eye. "I hope they get the whole bloody lot."

Llewellyn chuckled at the thought too. "I'd take the encyclopaedia of world diseases and give it to them for breakfast, lunch and supper. Let them have the lot."

After a time, the shoreline bore west and it became apparent to Blanc that they had gone around in a half circle in order to keep to the low ground's cover. Again, they could hear the swarms of flies and see the noisy crows before the first corpses appeared at the bridge. Handkerchiefs were put across faces to guard against the rotting stench, and all looked to one another briefly contemplating. An unpleasant task awaited them. In unison they all moved forward walking around the bloated and festering dead. One French sailor called Bisset picked up a rifle and looked triumphant with his find.

Blanc, knowing that it was useless without ammunition, instructed the young sailor to quickly search the dead man's ammunition pouches.

Instantly Bisset's face changed to one of disgust. He hesitated and Blanc gently scolded the youngster to get a grip and reminded him of the bad things they had overcome to still be alive.

Lewis went ahead, disturbed by the carnage. Many of the corpses were burnt, black-boned skeletons from the heat ray. "These poor souls never had a chance. They must have been caught out here with nowhere to run except Eastend. Look – some are on the bridge and others are lying on the mud banks on the other side."

Blanc stood next to him. "You can see that they tried to run in a futile effort to get to the village."

Llewellyn called out. "Oh, my word! There is an artillery piece. It has rolled off the bridge onto the bank."

They all crossed the bridge and found the small cannon laying upon its side. It was by two dead horses, which were partially scorched and stiff in the wet mud, but the field gun looked fine. It's barrel above the mud and dry.

"I wonder if we can use that," suggested Blanc in a tone of excitement.

Lewis had pulled a small paper manual from an open box among the scattered litter.

"It's an instruction manual. The gun is called an Ordinance BL 5-inch howitzer." He looked up. "It sounds impressive." He looked at a large wooden crate of shells close by. He read the side label allowed. "These look like big bad boys. It says 50 lb Lyddite shells. What are Lyddite shells?"

"Lyddite," repeated Lefebvre. He could not speak English but he seemed to know what Lyddite meant in the context of artillery shells. He looked at Blanc and said: "Melinite." Then shrugged his shoulders.

Lewis continued to look at the booklet. "It says three-motion breech. Do you chaps know what that means?"

Blanc nodded his head and replied. "Yes, Lewis, I understand the gun. I am certain I will know how to load and fire such a weapon."

"Well, that sounds champion to me. Can we take it to Paglesham Churchend? It's only across the fields. We might get a chance to bash one of these Lyddite shells into the fighting machine. If it is still there. And I think it is." Lewis had a wicked glint in his eyes.

Blanc looked concerned. "These men lying about dead were trained soldiers. They never got the opportunity to fire such a shell when the fighting machines came."

"Perhaps we will have a better chance," replied Lewis. "Our one is damaged and I don't think others are likely to come. They are dying, I'm certain of it."

"This may be so, Lewis. The Martians are dying. However, they will not go quietly, my friend."

"We have no horses to pull the field gun," answered Llewellyn, watching the French sailors milling around the overturned gun.

Lewis was quick to add. "We could get the gun upright and wheel it to Paglesham Churchend. We would have to risk cutting across the field. Surely we could push it that short way. The wheels seem fine."

Blanc beamed with enthusiasm. "If there is one of these Martian things in the village, you might get one shot at it." He looked about and saw several long wooden boxes. "We must take a number of the 50lb shells."

Llewellyn was beginning to get nervous. "Are you lot sure? You'll only get one shot. The tripod will come after you before you can reload and get a second one off. The one shot will have to be a good one."

Lewis was more optimistic. "If we could find the Martian thing and get up close without it seeing us, we could fire one shot and scatter in different directions."

Blanc looked confused. "Scatter in different directions?"

"Oh, it'll come for us, mark my words," answered Llewellyn. "Look, I'm not so sure about this."

"It is only a small field gun. If we take it close to the village, it might be of use. We could get close to this fighting machine if it is there. We will not antagonise the creature within, if there is no need," said Blanc reassuringly. "I'm hoping this Martian thing is not there. The people you seek are well and greet us. I hope the Martian machine would move on."

"I don't think the fighting machine has gone elsewhere, Mister Blanc," replied Lewis. "They are colossal. I'm just surprised we have not seen further signs of the thing. They can hardly hide. However, there is a line of trees from the woods and the poplars along in the roadway as you enter the village. There is also the church with its belfry. That is hidden from view by the trees. The tripod machines do stand still for long periods of time."

"Perhaps it has just stopped," added P.C. Llewellyn. "You said they have been doing such things, Lewis. This one looked sluggish too."

"I agree with you, Mister Llewellyn." Blanc then turned to Lewis. "I also agree with what you say too, Lewis. Therefore, this big machine must be standing close to something that would hide it. Trees perhaps, or the church tower."

Lewis nodded. "There are many trees in Paglesham, and there are also woods obscuring our approach."

"Obscuring?" asked Blanc.

"It is another word meaning to hide or conceal," added Llewellyn.

"Oh, yes. Now I see. This is good. We can push the gun and remain obscure towards this wood." Blanc then turned to his men and asked in French. "We must bring the shells with the artillery piece?"

There were several replies of agreement. Lefebvre and a sailor called Segal lifted the crate of shells and wedged it upon the howitzer. The group seemed relieved by the prospect of a small artillery piece, something they could fire. It was a crude plan, but a plan none the less. The men were getting enthusiastic. A good sign in a forsaken land.

Blanc held up a finger to emphasise his point. "If we do use this artillery piece, we would need to be very close, Mister Policeman Llewellyn. Very close indeed, and our aim must be true with the first shot. I know the fighting machines can be crippled or destroyed by a well-placed shell. I have seen them hit. But not by small artillery like this."

"I hope so too. Believe me, Mister Blanc! You don't shoot at those enormous blighters and let them know where you are." P.C. Llewellyn was getting decidedly agitated.

"I should go on ahead and scout the place," added Lewis. "I'll signal from the woodland before Churchend. That way I can let you know if it is safe to bring the gun across the fields."

"I'll instruct two of my men to accompany you." Blanc turned and called in French. "Laurent and Bisset. You will go with this man. Stay with him at all times." Blanc pointed at Lewis.

Laurent and Bisset nodded glumly. The French sailors looked unsure of being alongside a foreign man who could not speak their language.

"Come on, then," smiled Lewis, still clutching his dead hares in one hand with the other firmly gripping his rifle strap across his torso. They left, heading towards the immediate derelict cottages of Paglesham Eastend, with Gippy following. Beyond was the large meadow of blotched pink and green, separating Eastend village from Paglesham Churchend – the other half of what had once been the Paglesham rural community.

Lewis's reconnoitring group left the others to the task of shifting the artillery piece from the ditch. Within moments further horrors faced them. The three men passed a small, decrepit boatyard that was devoid of boats. More decomposing soldiers lay scattered about. The buzzing of flies and the smell of human putrefaction caused them to gag. Rotten corpses were scattered along the path. It was obvious the dead soldiers had been trying to run. Their withering, blackened forms were twisted in ugly positions. Quickly, Lewis and his two companions passed the wretched forms and made their way along a shingle path with high hedgerows. Here, unhealthy red weed still clung to the natural greenery. Lewis remembered the red weed looking much more vibrant, and he took more pleasure in its decline. When they came to the end of the track, before them were terraces of small fisherman's cottages. They were stained black with alien soot, a product of the black, poisonous gas that had been dispersed by the Martians. Around the walls were more dead soldiers, again covered in black soot. They had died in the same diabolical and twisted attitudes, agonising in their wretched death throes.

"They fumigated the cottages," muttered Lewis, looking to the two French sailors with him. Laurent made a sign of the cross as they quickened their pace. Each man wanted to be beyond the hideous stench of death and out in the field, where the fresh breeze was full of crisp, clean air. Air that no longer had the sweet, sickening smell of red weed.

⇌⇋

Back on the mud banks, the other members of the group heaved away at the field gun using some old discarded oars that they had found. All things were put to good use. After a few creaks of protest, the gun was lifted and rolled unceremoniously onto its undamaged wheels.

"Oh, très bien," replied Blanc. Keeping his men occupied and focused was helping all.

"Good men, very good," applauded P.C. Llewellyn. "Let's get it through the village then, boys."

Blanc smiled and patted him on the shoulder. "Your enthusiasm is reborn, Constable – this is good." Once again, Blanc broke off from English and spoke to his men in French. "Is that crate of shells firmly wedged in? We do not want them falling along the way."

"They are firmly in place, Quartermaster," replied Lefebvre.

The French sailors gathered around the field gun. Two lifted it by the spade at the rear. The barrel was aimed at the ground. Then other men began to push and turn the wheels of the gun forward. First across the bridge and then towards an opening in the pink-smothered hedgerow. They steered the howitzer through the gap and onto the patchy green and pink field. They could see Lewis, Bisset and Laurent far ahead, approaching the woods on the other side of the field. Lewis was waving back at them to proceed across the field.

"We will be making for the tall bush line to the right," advised Llewellyn. "Where you can see the tops of the poplar trees beyond. If we keep moving to the right, we'll come to a stile that leads to the church graveyard. We must get close to the bush line first, then move along using it as cover. We can remain hidden from the fighting machine if it is there. I'm presuming it is." He looked about. "If it had gone elsewhere, we would surely see the blasted thing."

"We noticed it early this morning from the boat. It was just before dawn," replied Blanc. "I believe it is around here somewhere. As you say, the fighting machines are very big. The trees, and perhaps a church tower, are the only things that could hide such a giant machine."

P.C. Llewellyn smiled nervously. "Well, I'm still hoping that the Martian is not there. But somehow, I think it will be. Even though it has not been moving about much. It must be ill. It would have gone or moved on by now."

Blanc thought the British bobby made an amusing picture in the apocalyptic landscape. He did not know which was the more bizarre; the eccentric British bobby being so wonderfully British in a crisis; or the pink and green patchwork fields in which he was being so wonderfully British. The strange artists of Paris might love to paint such a picture. He grinned kindly at the likeable policeman.

"We shall see, Policeman Constable Llewellyn, we shall see."

Llewellyn liked Blanc's approach. There was a gritty fire in the old quartermaster. It was as though he thought he could perform miracles with the small gun. This clearly inspired confidence among his men.

"Well, Mister Blanc, I've always regarded myself as a rather cautious person. One who never takes unnecessary risks…"

Blanc smiled and held up his hand, his finger pointing to the sky. "That has all changed,

Policeman Llewellyn. It changed when the Martians invaded. You have taken bold decisions and a number of risks. You are a survivor, Sir. And a very good one. So is your friend Lewis. But you need to find this Mrs Steed and her family. Well, we cannot do this without risk. Caution is now an empty cup, Sir."

P.C. Llewellyn pondered the words. Reluctantly, he nodded his head in agreement. What else could he do? He was beginning to form the idea that Blanc was one of those old adventurers. This was fine. But Llewellyn realised he had to go on this adventure with the French seaman and his remaining crew mates. He doubted Blanc had much idea how colossal and imposing the Martian fighting machines were at close range. Once again, Llewellyn looked at the small artillery piece and decided it looked insufficient against the fighting machines. But he also knew Blanc was uninterested in such assumptions. Blanc did not want his men to know of such pessimistic things either. Perhaps he was carried away by what he had seen when hundreds of huge naval guns had bombarded the coastline. Multitudes of bigger and more powerful guns, concentrated on one target.

P.C. Llewellyn was sweating. He gave Blanc an anxious smile and raised his eyebrows. "Very well, Mister Blanc. We'll do it your way. I don't have a plan. You have something of an insurance plan. I'm not sure the premium payments are up to scratch, but I suppose it is better than nothing."

Blanc could only understand that there was compliance expressed in the policeman's words, though he was a little lost on the imagery. "Très bien, Policeman Llewellyn. Très bien indeed." He thought the 'indeed' sounded wonderfully British.

Llewellyn grinned too. Secretly, he wished he had just ridden into the village on his bike first. He should have left the French sailors for later.

CHAPTER 6

THE HORROR IN THE CHURCH

Reg froze with fear as the small door beneath the stairs creaked. A chill ran up his spine, and goose bumps began to form on his thick arms. He licked his lips nervously and stared at young Jimmy.

Jimmy whispered fearfully. "Be careful, Uncle. We don't want the Martian to hear us."

"I know, Jimmy," his uncle replied in his usual slow manner. "Shush now and listen. We will hear the thing if it starts to move."

For some minutes they strained their ears, but there was nothing save the wind that swept across the fields to the rear of the cottage and the rustling of the poplar trees out in the front. Inside, the public house was silent as could be expected from a deserted place. The interior had become dusty, but apart from that, things were rather tidy. Old furniture and ornaments but neat. Mister and Mrs Walker had been house-proud people.

"Are you sure that Mister Walker kept a shotgun in here?" Jimmy was reluctant to persist with the squeaky door.

"I'm very sure, Jimmy. Mum told me never to touch guns. But sometimes Lewis and Mister Walker took me poaching with them. Very early in the morning, on Saturdays. It was when Mum and you took the cart into Rochford to get groceries. Mister Walker had several guns and I'm sure he could not have given them all away."

"I can't imagine Nan letting you go poaching with Lewis. Nanny doesn't approve of him. She thinks he's a rascal."

"Oh, er – yes, you would be right about that Jimmy. She never knew. God! She would have gone mad if she found out." Then Reg grinned like a naughty boy. "But it was great fun. I rather liked Lewis." There was a tone of remorse for the man's absence. "Mum said: 'despite his misgivings and what other well to do folk think of Lewis, they were happy to buy a pheasant or rabbit from him.'" Reg could always use big words when quoting his mother, though he was not always sure of their meaning.

"So, Nanny did like him?" Jimmy was confused.

"Well, Mum said he were all right in small doses. Mum also thought other folk were hypo..." He stopped trying to remember the rest of the word.

"Hypocrites," corrected Jimmy.

"Oh aye, that's it, she called them that." He lifted the cellar door beneath the stair case, before gently easing it open. To their delight and relief, there was no squeak.

"Can you see anything, Uncle," whispered Jimmy as he watched his giant, dim-witted uncle leaning into the stair closet.

Reg moved carefully backwards away from the closet door holding a double-barrel shotgun and a bag full of cartridges. Upon his face was a radiant smile. The look of excited success. "Don't touch now, Jimmy, I'm going to lean this here while I get something else out of there."

"What is it, Uncle," Jimmy asked excitedly.

"There is another shotgun. A single-barrelled one." Again, he emerged with thrilled expression. "And this," he added with grim menace as his jaw locked fiercely. He had a small hand-held scythe. His eyes blazed as though a new found power had come to him. "Oh, I would love to get me a swipe at one of them Martian things outside of their machine. Just to catch one out in the open and not so high and mighty in its fighting machine."

"Would you chop it up, Uncle?" Jimmy could feel his adrenalin running, knowing that his uncle could do serious damage to anything that was flesh and blood. "Oh, how I would love to see one of them Martians scream and squeal, Uncle. Especially if it was the one who took Nanny from us."

Reg stared down at his nephew and smiled, putting away the thoughts of revenge as quickly as they had come. "First, Jimmy, we load the guns. Lewis showed me how to do this and I must tell you also because these things are very dangerous if you do not carry them proper. They taught me this too."

"Lewis showed you how to use guns too? Good job Nanny did not find out. You would have been for it. Lewis too, no doubt."

Putting the scythe down, Reg unlocked the gun so that the single barrel dropped down from the stock. He then rummaged into the bag of shells and pulled one out, which he fitted into the back hollow of the barrel. "Now, Jimmy," he whispered. "We must leave the barrel hanging down and do not pull trigger back until we lock. We only lock when we get into the church, and only pull the catch back when ready to fire. These things can go off easily. We must not cause an accident to one of us."

"Is that one for me, Uncle?" Jimmy was awestruck by the implement. His own gun.

"Yes, Jimmy, but you must learn how to walk with it and use it properly. So please listen to me well. Lewis said he would drum this into my head time and time again before he would ever let me use one."

"So, Lewis let you use one?"

"Yes! But he always watched over me. He said it wasn't right to treat me like a child all the time like other folks did. Mister Walker did say so too."

"Where did he let you use it?"

"Down by the river banks further out so none would know. I shot a duck once, but he always told me to res…" Again, he could not remember the word.

"Respect," suggested Jimmy.

"Oh aye, that's it, respect the gun and carry it properly. Barrel unlocked and no cartridge in the barrel."

"But you have put a cartridge in the barrel." Jimmy wanted to point out the mistake.

"Oh aye, but that were when we were hunting ducks. Martians is bloody different, matey. I bet Lewis would have put a shell in the barrel. We only have to lock, pull the catch back and we are ready to fire, like this. We are going to be shaking and frightened."

Jimmy asked. "We might take too much time putting the shell into the barrel with shaky hands?"

"Aye, that's it, Jimmy."

"So, we are not going to do it like Lewis instructed?"

"No," Reg retorted, with shocked amazement. "When dealing with Martians, Lewis can go for a long walk about the shell not in the barrel bit."

Carefully he went through his instructions to his nephew and instilled into him that they would sneak towards the church with their loaded shotgun barrels hanging unlocked from the stocks. Upon reaching the church grounds, they would lock them and then enter the church.

After all was clear, they moved to the front door with weapons at the ready, as they had rehearsed. Gingerly, Reg turned the door lock and slowly opened it. The sound of the rustling poplar trees intensified, invading the hallway and calming each naive adventurer with nature's sound.

"Come," he whispered to his nephew. They cautiously stepped out and pressed themselves against the front of the public-house wall. A twelve-year-old boy trying to be brave, and a mentally challenged man trying to protect his nephew and find his mother. Each was trying to survive in a world where human life had become worthless, insignificant before inhuman monsters from another planet.

Reg moved in front of his nephew and crouched down low to whisper. "Follow me, Jimmy, and do exactly as I do, understand?"

"I understand, Uncle." His heartbeat was quickening as adrenalin and fear mixed in an intoxicating drive through his pumping veins. He felt bold with his single-barrel shotgun, and his uncle looked very imposing with his double-barrels and scythe.

Together they moved forward along the terrace of cottages towards the churchyard wall. Both stooped behind the old boulder wall as they reached it, stealthily moving onwards passed the gate entrance towards the huge, victoriously green, shrub line at the rear of the church. Here, most of the red weed was gone. Only a small stile, still covered in pinking weed offered an entrance through the contrasting green foliage. They nimbly took advantage of this.

They were then upon a small area of heath that ran on towards shingle from the river. The tide was out, exposing mud and sand banks. There were a few gulls that squalled, indifferent to the blight that had befallen the land. Moving a little way along the line of lined shrubs, Reg stopped and gently laid his gun upon the long red weed.

"There is an opening under here. I made it when I was a kid," said Reg as he knelt down and forced his way into the thicket. When he returned he whispered: "Pass me your gun and then mine, Jimmy."

The youngster quickly complied and then followed his uncle through the tunnelled bushes into the graveyard at the rear of the church. They were behind a large tombstone staring at the back of the partially obscured fighting machine. The gigantic alien machine was just standing there, an enormous and dilapidated structure against the tower.

The Last Days of the Fighting Machine

The belfry obscured its near side flank. At the rear, they could just make out the bottom of a cage. It was fixed upon the machine's rear spherical summit. It was a terrifying waiting place before the wretched prisoners had their blood sucked out while still alive.

"Why is it just standing there?" murmured Jimmy his heart pounding.

Reg frowned as he scrutinised the machine. "I think it is empty," he answered softly after some deliberation.

"Then are the Martian things are in the church?"

Reg did not respond. "Follow me, Jimmy."

He moved forwards, keeping the building between himself and the titanic machine, using the machine's rear and, what Reg supposed, the blind side for cover.

Young Jimmy was at his uncle's heels like a little shadow. Fearful, but keen. Lost in youthful naivety. They were doing something to confront his grandmother's abductors and killers. He could not help noticing things that were still there. Like the old workmen's scaffold board lying along the church wall, and how the old vicar had been vexed by the negligence of the workmen for forgetting it. Such matters were trivial when they were trying to retrieve his grandmother's body, maybe avenge her death. If the Martian creatures were not inside the machine, maybe he and Reg could find Granny's body? Jimmy could not say why, but he fancied his uncle was right about the gigantic insect-like machine being empty. He thought of the strange platform that went from the machine's trunk to the belfry window. He followed his uncle around the tower and looked up at the underbelly of the machine. Huge worm-like tentacles hung limply from a hatchway above his head. He shuddered, remembering having seen the whipping appendages pick people up. He had seen them wrap around the Walkers on that dreadful night when a fighting machine last came to Paglesham Churchend.

They were taking an enormous risk, but he was blindly following his uncle. Any well-meaning citizen would have screamed abuse at them. But the people were all gone now. It was just Uncle Reg and him.

They passed under the machine and around the huge tripod legs. Relieved, they turned the corner at the front of the church and looked out at the dry mud village road. Gingerly, they approached the porch. The stone-covered Norman archway led to the entrance door. For a moment they paused in the dark porch, panting with fear and allowing themselves a brief moment to capture their breath. Before them was the more dreadful part of their quest. Reality was slowly beginning to dawn through the adolescent cloud that had brought them to entrance.

Reg took a deep breath as he looked down at his flushed and sweating nephew. The youngster's eyes were wide with fear and his chest heaved in and out. But there was also a look of no turning back.

"It's now or never, Jimmy."

"Yes, Uncle, but careful. No bursting in. We have to go in and not let the Martians know we are coming. Our best thing is surprise. I think the creatures will be in there." He looked at his shotgun. It gave him a small feeling of reassurance.

"You are right, Jimmy," Reg murmured. "Give me your gun and I'll lock it for you. From now on, you must be very cautious and keep the gun at the ready. Remember to pull back the clip for firing."

Delicately, Reg locked the barrel of his nephew's gun before doing the same with his. The noise was minimal, as Mister Walker had always had the weapons well oiled. The old publican had also devised ways of lowering the noise when hunting, in order not to scare off prey before he had a chance to fire.

Reg smiled at his clever, brave little nephew. Carefully, he opened the door a mere fraction. It was just enough for him to squeeze through followed by Jimmy. Then he gently closed the door. Inside, neither dared to whisper amid the old walls where the slightest of sounds would be amplified by the acoustics of the aged stone curves that held up the roof. They looked about the nave and all the benches. It seemed undisturbed.

Putting his finger to his mouth, Reg pointed to the rear archway. It had a closed door that led to the stairs of the church tower.

The old arched, stain-glassed windows cast shafts of light from clear blue of the late summer morning. It was an eerie display, like funnelled spider's webbing, breaking through the gloom, enhancing the uncanny atmosphere. The dusty pews seemed to scream empty silence. The church was sterile, gothic grotto, long devoid of a congregation.

Jimmy swallowed. Once again, he looked at the dark, empty benches, straining to hear the sermons from his memory. He wanted to visualise the villagers in more congenial times. Fear lay in the pit of his stomach, and he began to ponder the dreadful consequences of being caught by the Martians. Horrific visions of Mrs Walker, screaming in abject terror flashed across his memory again. The horror was still screaming in his mind. Perhaps somewhere, the abominations were observing them. Making plans to attack. He battled to quash such gruesome reminiscences of the Walkers.

His uncle's huge hand rested upon his shoulder and squeezed firm reassurance into him. Enough to fuel the last drops of courage and resolve inside. For a moment, Uncle Reg was the light of ill-deserved confidence. Yet, all the same, it was assurance. Jimmy imagined the morbid shadows receding in awe.

Both gingerly crept across the stone floor to the inner arched entrance. Carefully opening the wooden door, slowly they peered in. Before them was a gloomy spiral stair case. One way went up. The other way went down into a crypt area. Their hearts pumped and hands sweated around the shotgun each held as they began to cautiously ascend. Their progress was slow and traumatic. Constantly, they would stop, hesitating before willing themselves on up into the dimness. The ghostly hush was becoming overpowering. But they had to battle with their frightened wits in silence. Finally, the light from the tower window brought them some relief. They looked to each other excitedly and moved a little quicker towards the arched window, stopping just before it. They knew they would be level and closer than ever to the body of the alien machine.

Again, Reg raised a finger to his lips, a signal to be quiet at all costs. Jimmy pushed his back to the wall, finding the rising tension almost too much to bear. He wanted to be out of the window's light. He breathed in through his nose and out through his mouth. Slowly, he began to calm himself. Enough to stay tolerant.

"Ooh!" Reg moaned in suppressed shock.

Jimmy almost jumped out of his skin. "Shush Uncle!" he whispered agitatedly.

"It's Mum," Reg murmured impatiently. "She's in the cage. She is alive."

"What! We must get her out."

Reg's firm arm shot out and kept Jimmy pinned to the wall. "We will," he muttered softly. "But first we think and look around. Mum has seen me and she knows we are here. She is hurt but I think she can move."

"Let me see her, Uncle. I'll be careful, I promise."

Reg released his arm and Jimmy very cautiously leaned past and peeped through the window over the dull-white, strange, shell-like alloy of the machine. There, by the smooth arced top, was the cage. Within lay his injured grandmother. Her long, mauve skirt was ripped and blood-stained, as was her white blouse. But what Jimmy found especially disturbing was the mass of congealed blood upon her forehead. Wisps of matted grey hair strands hung loosely from her bun. Granny's feminine elegance was battered and dishevelled. She always wore her hair pinned up and neat. From below, he and Uncle Reg could only make out the under floor of the meshed cage. That is why they had not been able to see her from the ground.

Her eyes widened in disbelief when she saw him and her lips mimed. "Jimmy."

Carefully, she raised herself. There was no top to the cage and even she could get out of it. However, there was nothing substantial for her to grip once out upon the smooth downward curved alloy of the machine. Anyone would slide off of the body trunk and fall to their death. There was a platform leading to the machine from the window's stone seal. Obviously used as a bridge by the alien to cross into the church tower. But it was too far from the cage for Reg or Jimmy to get access to the trapped woman.

She called softly to him. "They are not in the machine. There were two off them and they went inside."

Reg came out onto the open window. "Where did they go Mum? We need to get you out." It was as though he was on the verge of crying. Somehow, he managed to pull himself together and started to look about for things of use.

"There was a scaffold board downstairs that the vicar got annoyed about when the workmen left it on the grounds. It was out by the wall." Jimmy's mind was ticking over. "If we put it on the Martian bridge and lent it over to the cage, Nanny might be able to crawl along it. It's only a short way and I am sure the board will be long enough."

"You stay with my Mum. I'm going to get it," Reg whispered.

"Uncle Reg, are you sure…"

"Stay with Nanny," asserted Reg. "Keep your gun ready and I'll be as quick as I can."

Reg sped off down the staircase as quickly as he could. His fear of the darkness was gone. He had other things to do, and apprehension had to go backstage in the theatre of his mind. Concern about the Martians was gone too. His mother had to be rescued, and that was a real possibility if he could move swiftly enough.

Jimmy gripped his shotgun for reassurance and waited by the window seal in view of his grandmother. She was now standing and looking less abject about her predicament. The sight of her son and grandson had lifted her. Suddenly, there was hope.

"Be careful, Jimmy. Two of them went inside some time ago," she hissed from the cage. "I think they went down the stairs, deeper into the church. I assume you and Uncle Reg did not see or hear them?"

"No, Granny. They were nowhere in the nave or among the benches. They may be in the vestry." He looked about nervously. His heart thumping with fear. Impatient anxiety began to make his hands tremble. "I can see Uncle Reg down below. He is outside now. He has got that scaffold board, Granny. We are going to get you out."

His grandmother smiled from her captivity. There were tears in her eyes. She was a picture of very mixed and conflicting emotions. "Keep that gun ready, Jimmy, and watch the stairs. Don't get over-excited and shoot your Uncle, now. Remember, he will be coming up them in a moment." She looked pitiable with her thin strands of hair hanging about her face, caked in congealed blood, and her shabby dress ripped and dirty.

Yet Jimmy realised his grandmother was showing evidence of the disciplined lady she was. The matriarch was returning, much to Jimmy's growing joy. He and Uncle Reg would need her resolve. She was always full of social correctness. The Martians had almost stripped her of that. But still she retained her sternness, even though she had been reduced to the appearance of a wild woman, as if she were a person who had never known any form of polite society.

For what seemed like an eternity, Jimmy waited, poised with the shotgun pointing at the stairs. He was terrified of standing about waiting for what would surely come. He was more horrified at the thought of leaving his poor grandmother. His heart leapt and he almost shot his Uncle Reg as he appeared with the scaffold board.

Once again, his uncle whispered to him to be quiet as he went passed and leaned the scaffold board on the window seal.

"I'm going out onto the bridge, Jimmy," he whispered. "I want you to slide the board out once I am in place." He looked at his nephew with clear stress etched upon his simple disposition.

"I will, Uncle," he replied quietly. "Let's do it now."

Reg squeezed his huge bulk through the small arched window of the bell tower and was nimbly out on the alien bridge. He had never feared heights and was sure footed as he made his way along the narrow fighting machine's span. There was a closed circular door. Here the platform slid out of an opening below and he shuddered if it might open or the platform was withdrawn into the machine, leaving him to fall.

"They are not inside the machine, Reggie. They went into the tower and down," whispered his mother from the cage.

Reg nodded with a confused frown. He looked again at the lifeless fighting machine, feeling less intimidated by the alien hulk. He could feel the breeze up high and could see for miles, but he was able to put the unstable elevation out of his simple mind. He would concentrate on the task of getting his mother out of the cage. He looked back to the window and could see Jimmy was already sliding the scaffold board out onto the Martian bridge.

Carefully, Reg bent down and lifted the panel, wobbling slightly as he adjusted his grip more firmly. Using his foot as a pivot he swung the other end of the board out at an angle of about thirty degrees and turned it in a circle from the arched bell tower window towards the cage. His mother was able to grip the end of it.

"Be careful, Reggie, I need to push it back towards you and then back to place it between these little bar things."

Reg was able to bring back his side of the board a little. Then his mother pulled the board towards her again. It fit snugly between the bars. The slant from the cage down to the Martian platform was extreme, but then their predicament was much more so. She would chance the extremity for all she was worth.

Reg had great faith in his mother. She was a lady of decisive ways, and wasted no time in nimbly climbing out of the cage and onto the board. Despite her age, she showed a great and agile sense of purpose. Suddenly, she no longer looked as helpless and frail as she did a few moments before. The old 'no nonsense' mother was back. Reg felt his own confidence grow in her presence. His foot was back in place to stop the board from sliding while his mother could cautiously grip and lower herself down the slanting scaffold board towards him.

To her son and grandson's great joy she slid a little and gripped with hands and legs. Then she repeated the awkward movement a few times more before Reg was able to get a firm grip of her. He helped her down the rest of the way.

She looked out at the panoramic view. She had been sitting in the cage a long time and the height was not causing the same dread anymore.

"Well done, Reggie."

She gave him a quick kiss and continued. "Now, let's get out of here." She walked to the arched window where her grandson waited anxiously for her. His face was a flood of tears and pleasure. He helped her in as quickly as possible. When she had jumped down before him, Jimmy hugged her. Reg followed in and picked up his shotgun, which was leaning against the wall.

"Let's be going, then," suggested Reg. "We need to get away from here, Mum."

As they turned to move down the dark stairway, they froze. From out of the gloom, a grotesque form shuffled upon the stairwell. Most of its form was hidden by shadow. There were limbed attachments slithering on either side of the staircase walls – an obscured, squid-like shape masked by the dimness, sensed rather than viewed.

Ughlaaaa!

A screech ripped through the air. The sound shook the floor. Mrs Steed and her family shuddered at the onslaught of the severe, high-pitched noise. Each felt their legs buckle. It was coupled with a brief and confusing image. The vague shape looked grey-skinned and multi-limbed. One such appendage shot forth and grabbed Jimmy. He was lifted and held dangling for a moment. As though the hidden form might be studying its prey.

Mrs Steed gasp with horror. Slowly Jimmy was being pulled down into the shadows of the stairwell. Towards the hideous outline. Frantically he kicked and struggled.

"No!" screamed his grandmother as she launched herself into the darkness and grabbed Jimmy's leg. "Leave him alone," she screamed. She lunged over her grandson's dangling form and punched the vile spongy flesh of the alien limb. She had conjured all her might. The alien emitted an ear-splitting squeal and released its grip. Mrs Steed and her grandson fell back against the wall of the stairwell. Reg stepped down passed them. He calmly raised his shotgun and fired both barrels down into the darkness. The point-blank boom and the flash smashed the darkness away. For a split second, there was an agonised screech and the sight of a huge grey mottled head on three legs, a huge mouth like a giant bird's beak. Open and shrill, ripping through the air with agonised pain! Then darkness reclaimed the scene. The hideous alien feelers were slithering back, and they could hear the monstrosity scuffling away, back down the dark stairs, screeching and yelping as it hurriedly retreated.

Frantically, Mrs Steed grabbed Jimmy's arm and pulled him up.

"Let's be out of here," she called and picked up the shotgun that Jimmy had dropped. She led the way down the steps. Reg and Jimmy followed. They could hear the retreating creature as it smashed out of the doorway at the bottom. It would be slithering across the nave now, trying to find cover.

Reg reloaded his shotgun with two were more shells as they charged down the stairwell. The family were roaring in anger to will themselves on; also to let the alien know they were game for the fight. As they burst through the lower door into the nave, they could see a thick trail of blood – red, like human blood. The Martian was out of sight but the blood trail led towards the pews, which were screeching aside or falling over. It was as though an angry and invisible poltergeist was throwing the furniture about. The creature must be crawling on the floor among the benches, scurrying, in panic, for the doorway on the further side of the nave.

"It is making for the vestry," said Mrs Steed. "Come on. Let's get out of here now. Put that thing away, Reggie."

Reggie was consumed with a blood lust. The animal instinct for survival had become ferocious. "We can't let it get back to the fighting machine, Mum. We can't stop it if it gets back in that thing."

"No, Reggie please leave this," she implored her son. When his temper was hot, Reg needed to be handled carefully. "Not now darling, please."

Reg had his shotgun in one hand and the scythe in the other. He moved forward, ignoring his mother's plea.

Frozen to the spot, Mrs Steed and her grandson watched, mesmerised with fear. Reg slowly followed the blood trail down the central walkway. He had a look of intense purpose as he turned into the displaced pews towards the front of the nave. His eye's widened, with a gleam of wicked delight. Amid the overturned pews, Reg halted before something amid the displaced benches. Mrs Steed and Jimmy knew it was the unseen, bloodied alien, hidden from their view. Only Reg could see it, grunting and whining. He knew the thing was afraid. For a moment, he looked down, silent, his jaw firmly locked, experiencing satisfaction. There was the sound of alien laboured breath, and it whimpered like a skewered hog. The others could only imagine its hidden face, looking up from the church floor while tentacles slowly pulled its bulk through the carnage of broken and displaced church pews. They could only imagine what Reg was looking down at.

Reg's grim look turned to revulsion as he stepped forward with his double-barrelled shotgun reloaded and a new look of vicious cruelty. Some of the alien's appendages were raised in a futile attempt at defence.

The creature tried to make a last-ditch attempt at retreat towards the dark doorway of the vestry. Reg's huge bulk followed as more pews were displaced. He was grinning with anger. His face was sweating but he retained a look of cold, determined purpose.

The tension for the two observers was overwhelming. Reg was beyond control. His mother knew it. She was resigned to letting her son do what he felt he must. She grasped Jimmy and pulled him close, hugging him tightly as Reg's first barrel fired. The boom shook the church. Another terrified and high-pitched alien shriek, the sound of a demon choking. Pathetic snorting filled the house of worship, like a banshee pleading from Hell. A second shot came, amid further vile and terrified squeals. The alien's high-pitched uproar was full of horrendous panic, while Reg roared a deep and booming below. He dropped the shotgun's barrels as the smouldering cartridges fell out. He reloaded. Took aim again. Another two rapid shots.

Boom – boom!

Blood and gore exploded above the displaced pews. A sequence of more choking shrieks. As if the alien was pleading. Did Martians plead?

Human fury was being unleashed, unabated. Mrs Steed and her grandson hugged and watched.

Reg reloaded. Another boom. Then another. The petrified alien had been too badly injured to defend itself. They watched Reg amid the fountains of exploding red gore from the displaced pews. They heard the pathetic screams of the creature as its torment gradually diminished to nothing. Then the ringing silence. The deed was done.

Grandmother and grandson clutched each other tightly, their faces pressed together in their desperate embrace. They had witnessed the grey alien appendages flaying helplessly above the displaced pews, feelers with three long thin fingers. They had looked ineffective and pathetic. It was a futile bid by an inhuman creature confronted by a human life form that was every bit as callous. The panic-stricken shrieks were gone, now succumbed to the constant, eerie silence that had fallen over the dead flesh. It had been pointless for the unwelcome and hated fiend to try and protect itself. Yet it had tried. Whatever the vulgar form looked like, only Reg knew.

"Reg, love. It's dead," said his mother. "You've killed it, Reg."

He was still lost in a womb of gorgeous and annihilating passion. Reg was in a place that he was reluctant to leave.

"Enough now, Reg. Please!" She was anxious to claim her son back. Back from his all-consuming anger.

Reg had lost his temper to combat the fear. On occasion, he had done so as a child. Often, he had been mocked. Others who had been cruel to him had witnessed the same focused and uncontrolled anger.

Mrs Steed and Jimmy watched in awestruck horror as Reg's shotgun clicked shut again. Reloaded, but not to fire at the dead monstrosity anymore. The Martian was truly dead. Yet the spiteful desire to mutilate still lingered. Reg wanted to continue shooting into lifeless alien flesh. But his mother's voice was able to stop him. He was a man reluctantly leaving a locked room; someone leaving the rage of merciless killing, deserting an immense, energising blood lust. Something had tried to take the two most precious things in his life. First his mother and then his nephew. For a time, Reg could not stop. He continued to stare at the pulped and brutish monstrosity. He had to put aside the frenzy to annihilate the thing. It had already been done.

"We can only try to stop him while he is like this," she murmured to Jimmy. "His temper is cooling. I can accept that he needed to burn this out of him. That thing is deserving of no sympathy at all."

They continued to watch as Reg just stared at what he had done. Soon, he was whimpering through clenched teeth as he began to slap the side of his head.

Gradually, his slapping slowed down. His anger abated until he could slap no more. He turned slowly to his mother, crying and gasping for breath, exhausted by the energy he had released in his frenzy. The gruesome testimony of his bloodletting was all over him. Thick red gore, like that of any mutilated Earth-type mammal.

"Reggie, we must go now, darling," whispered his mother softly. "You've done well and you got the wicked sod."

Suddenly, Jimmy started to gag and shake. Mrs Steed and Reg turned to him. They feared the youngster might be having an epileptic fit.

"Jimmy, no, please," said his uncle, now back to his senses. "It's all right."

The young boy was reaching for breath and pointing to the stairwell. The stairs to the very tower they had been in and emerged from moments ago. His grandmother turned to look, while Reg tried to reassure his nephew.

"It's all right Jimmy – its dead now."

As Mrs Steed peered into the darkness of the rising stairs, a flicker of movement caught her attention. She saw the silhouette or shadow of spider like appendages gripping the walls and ceiling. The second outrageous thing was barely recognisable. All were unable to make out a complete image of the thing. It receded away back up the stairwell.

"It's the other one," said Mrs Steed. "I knew there were two of them."

One of the Martian's limbs was still slithering along the staircase wall. The attachment retreating after the main creature's absconded form.

Mrs Steed impulsively grabbed Jimmy's single-barrelled shotgun. With grim determination, she quickly took aim and fired. The bang was deafening, and there was an agonised scream. Blood and tissue exploded where the pellets hit. They heard the alien fiend scamper off up the winding staircase.

As the echo abated and the cordite receded, Jimmy gulped and began to breathe properly again. "Can we get out of here?" he pleaded nervously.

"Yes, Jimmy," replied his grandmother. She helped him to his feet.

Reg looked up as he heard a thud outside. It sounded like a door clamping shut.

"It is back in the fighting machine," said Reg.

"Oh, my God!" shouted Mrs Steed.

They heard the whirr of the alien machine start up and the scaffold board fall.

"Get out now," Mrs Steed screamed in panic. At once they all ran to the main door. "It's in the machine!"

They fled outside through the porch and down the side of the church. The fighting machine's whirring machinery was louder than ever. The three fugitives ran across the graves towards the high hedgerow and scrambled through into the ditch on the opposite side. As they all slid down into the trench, each looked back between the pink and green hedgerow, panting to get their breath. They gulped in fear at the creak of huge grinding metallic joints.

Reg was now shaking with anxiety. He wanted his anger back. "Oh Christ! Here comes the bugger, Mum."

From the blind side of the church tower, the colossal tripod's huge limbs buckled outwards. From the top of these limbs, upper limbs hung back down from elbow-like joints. This allowed the top upper limbs to cradle the body casing. Now the machinery grinded into motion. The alien body trunk lifted amid the grating and protesting sound of hydraulics. The attachments heaved like a three-limbed weight lifter. Slowly, the grinding and protesting canopy's mass elevated. As the body trunk lifted, an array of appendages moved: dancing tentacles, one holding the cylindrical device that fired the dreadful heat ray. Soon the canopy was just above the church tower's spire. The light grey alloy of the machine's undercarriage wickedly gleamed against the clear blue sky.

Alughhhh!

The machine's usual war cry fanned out across the pink and green countryside.

Alooo-ughh!

It roared again as it took a gigantic pace away from the church. The thud of its heavy tread shook the earth. For a moment the fighting machine wobbled, as though not sure of its footing, or perhaps the controller was too weak to control the machine properly.

"It is trying to steady itself," said Reg.

"There's something wrong with it," whispered Jimmy. "It has no sure footing."

"Quiet now, Jimmy," scolded his grandmother.

They watched on petrified as the giant machine stepped around the tower to stand in the graveyard. The ground trembled with each of the three legs' pounding steps. It stopped monetarily before the church entrance and tilted its trunk down. Again, there was the sound of protesting and grinding hydraulics. A spinal cord rose above the trunk with the pipe attachment at the end. A canister shot out. It smashed through the roof tiles.

"Get down low," hissed Reg. "It's putting black smoke into the church."

"It must think we are still in there. It's trying to flush us out," his mother replied. She looked to her grandson. "Come on. Jimmy, we are getting out of here. We'll make to the stile and head to the woods and fields on the way to Eastend."

Aloo ughh!

Again, the tripod boomed out its war cry as three tentacles sprang out from its body trunk. Two smashed through the stained-glass windows, and the third pierced the old wooden door.

"No black smoke is coming from the windows," muttered Jimmy as he turned to look imploringly at his grandmother. "It doesn't have any black smoke left."

He began to look excited, but his grandmother cut him short and pushed him on.

"Not now, Jimmy, let's get away from here. For God's sake, move, young man!"

All three stealthily crept back towards the stile, cautiously climbed got over it, and hid behind the church wall. They had to use the stone barrier for cover while sneaking past the machine, which was preoccupied with searching inside the church.

Fighting back the fear that was throbbing in every vein, they edged themselves on to their cottage – the first, next door to the holy grounds and at the end of the village terrace. Once behind the cover of the buildings, they quickly sped along the deserted houses. No one had any intention of hiding in their home. They fled past the upturned horse cart and made for the small woods just outside the village. They were almost within the confines of the trees when they heard the heat ray spew its deadly fire into the old church.

There was a colossal boom, which lifted them from their feet and slammed them down upon the muddy track. Each of them was winded by the fall.

Reg turned to see a huge fireball climbing into the clear blue sky, with huge boulders falling in all directions. The windows and the roof slates blew up and out from the terrace of old cottages. The tiles had neatly lifted like an elongated wave before falling in disarray into thousands of pieces. The debris rained all about. Instinctively, the three curled into a protective ball amid the cascading wreckage.

Dusty and dishevelled, Reg reached for his mother, who was coughing and spluttering. Jimmy had already stood sneezing, and pathetically trying to dust himself down.

"Into the woods now, boys – quickly!"

Mrs Steed's matriarchal voice was primed. She was fixed in her desire to protect her family. She was covered with scratches and a fresh layer of dust as she clutched the single-barrelled shotgun. Her dirty blood-matted hair was buried beneath the new layer of dust. The congealed blood on her already injured forehead lent her a savage appearance. But she still had sharp presence of mind and the nimbleness of a woman much younger than her fifty-five years.

She followed Reg and Jimmy into the sanctuary of the little wood, going deep into its centre to lay low.

Aloooughh!

The booming call tore out across the landscape and they heard the earth shaking. The machine was striding down the muddy lane, smashing through the line of tall poplar trees to halt before the wood they had just entered.

Everything went silent. All three held their breath, shaking with fear. They pressed themselves against the trees. What would come next? How could they escape from this predicament?

CHAPTER 7

TERROR OF THE WOODS

Lewis and his two companions instinctively went to ground when they heard the shotgun go off. It was at that moment they first glimpsed the distant trunk of the fighting machine by the church tower. They might have missed it, standing so close to a familiar piece of architecture. It was almost camouflaged against the old church. The machine had even lowered its structure to fit comfortably next to the old belfry.

"That shot came from inside the church. It has to be the Steed family," muttered Lewis.

Laurent and Bisset could not understand exactly what Lewis was saying, but they knew enough to fathom that all was not well.

For a few minutes they remained still and hidden. Each man was watching carefully. Then a second shotgun boomed within the church.

"That was a different blast from the first. There are two guns," muttered Lewis.

"Look!" Bisset said in French as he pointed to the belfry. Something diabolical had emerged from a window onto a platform leading to the fighting machine. The creature was distant – hard to decipher and moving quickly. It resembled a giant butter bean that had turned a grotesque grey. Three thick appendages served as legs. These limbs part walked and part slithered on the conduit to the fighting machine from the belfry window. A multitude of thinner tentacles gripped the tripod machine while others clung to the church tower. The thin limbs looked like a swiftly moving bundle of support rigging. Suddenly, the flaying alien arms let go of the stonework to help pull the body closer to the unmoving machine. Then the Martian was gone, into the machine.

Lewis frowned as he took in that fleeting glimpse. The tripods were made in the crude image of the Martians. Three legs with multiple whip-like appendages to grab and pick things up.

They watched in horrified disbelief as the fighting machine whirred into life. The contraption creaked and groaned as it raised itself to full height.

This time Laurent pointed and cursed in French, as they made out the figures of Mrs Steed, Reg and Jimmy fleeing the church towards the hedgerows.

The machine boomed out its battle cry before circling the medieval church with a few huge strides.

It smashed through the roof and doorway to search inside with its many tentacles.

Lewis and his companions pushed forward along the hedgerow ditch and then bolted across the last stretch of open ground, one at a time to reach the cover of the small copse of trees. Gippy had been following but now she lingered hesitantly before the small open field from hedgerow ditch to the woods.

Lewis frantically waved to her from the woodland fringes. "Come on, girl. Come now, there's a good girl." He had quite neglected the poor little mutt, which was clearly terrified by the immense moving structure in the distance. "Come, girl. Please!"

Finally, Gippy plucked up courage and shot out of the hedgerow and scampered into the field as fast as her little legs could carry her. She had just got half way across when the unconcerned fighting machine fired its heat ray into the old church and blew the building apart in a ball of angry high rising flame. Debris lifted into the clear blue sky and then cascaded down and about the small village. The force of the blast knocked Gippy onto her side. She yelped in pain and was thrown into a roll. As all the wreckage came down, Gippy stood. She began yelping hysterically and dancing in circles, as though trying to chase her tail.

Bisset ran past Lewis to go to the little dog's rescue, much to the old poacher's protests.

"No! For God's sake no."

Laurent stood beside Lewis and asked. "Ce qui a tort?"

"Your mate as gone out after the dog," he pointed at Bisset running out into the field.

Bisset was sentimental. He reached the yelping terrier and picked her up. The debris had stopped falling and as the dust and smoke cleared, he noticed that the machine had turned. Possibly, the Martian had heard Gippy's barking. Its trunk appeared to be tilted, as though the green-orbed window was looking down into the open field. Bisset and Gippy were clearly in the machine's line of vision.

"Oh God, the thing has seen him," said Lewis nervously. "Run," he hissed to Bisset through clenched teeth. "Run man! Run for your life."

Bisset needed no second bidding. He bolted back towards the woods with Gippy clutched against him. His other hand firmly gripping his rifle.

Alloo-ugh!

The fighting machine boomed out its all too familiar war cry. It tore through the air and the rustling leaves, then strode towards the line of poplars in the middle of the village road way. It stopped at the other side of the wooded copse, where it knew the fleeing sailor had gone.

Within the woods, Lewis was hissing his contempt at young Bisset's stupidity. "You fool," he hissed in frustration and anger. "Now we are all in danger and that thing will flush us out. Christ, what possessed you to be so blooming foolish?"

The young Frenchman looked down remorsefully. Although he could not understand Lewis, he guessed that he had compromised them by his rash actions.

They crept deeper into the woods searching for a hiding place. To Lewis it seemed futile, but doomed sheep still look for a secluded corner and were waiting in a flock before inevitable death. As they walked between the trees, he was surprised by the sight of Mrs Steed huddled behind a tree with her terrified son and grandson. Why he should be so astounded when he had seen them escape, he could not say, but he was uplifted to know they had made it to the woods – a minor respite despite the dreadfulness of their predicament. He grinned at Mrs Steed. Her dust-covered face and matted locks were stiff with congealed blood. Yet she still had that usual determined look in her face.

"Just had your hair done?" He thought a light hearted joke better than nothing.

"Yes, Mr Puttnam. And I want my bloody money back," she spat back angrily.

"We've been looking for you," he replied as he knelt down before them.

"Well, if you have a way out, I'm all ears, Mister Puttnam." She never called him Lewis. Her formal address to him was a mark of disfavour and she had never wanted to be on friendly terms with the poacher, despite an inkling of grudging respect for his uncompromising way of life.

He grinned through sad eyes. "That thing knows we are in here and soon the black smoke will be choking us out." He looked up into the green leaves that had no parasitic red weed.

"It hasn't got any black smoke," replied Jimmy.

Lewis frowned. "What do you mean it hasn't got…?"

The dishevelled Mrs Steed cut in. "The fighting machine is out of black smoke. That's why it blew up the church. It fired in a canister and nothing came out. No more poisonous gas." She looked back through the trees nervously then turned to Lewis. "It searched with its tentacles and then blew the place up with its heat ray. We had got out and sneaked here. We thought we had not been noticed, but it would seem we were wrong."

"The thing saw us entering the woods from the other side in the field after it blew up the church."

"Well, it will search with its tentacles and then if it finds nothing it will burn out the wood." Reg said morbidly.

The two French sailors looked up and around nervously, expecting something to come crashing through the trees. Lewis looked at Laurent and Bisset and signalled them to lay low. Each complied, trying to fathom what Lewis and Mrs Steed were saying to each other.

"We have five more French seamen and P.C. Llewellyn coming here with a small field gun. They found it at the old makeshift bridge at the boatyard in Eastend.

"Was it the one on its side by the mud bank next the dead horses?" asked Jimmy.

Lewis nodded. "If we can hold out for a while, they might get the big gun across the field and be able to get off an artillery shot into the thing."

"They'll be seen a mile off rolling a cannon across an open field." Jimmy moaned.

"Not if they come along the river bank and up by the old stile."

They all jumped nervously at the sound of creaking alloy overhead. Then there was a thunderous, earth-shattering boom as the machine's huge foot smashed down through the trees at the fringes of the wood from where Lewis and his two French companions had come. All scattered for the cover of bush and trees, while Gippy huddled up against the French sailor who had saved her.

"What's happening," stuttered Mrs Steed as she pulled Jimmy close.

The Last Days of the Fighting Machine

"The thing is straddling the woods," whispered Lewis as another foot smashed through the foliage towards the western edge of the wood.

From above came the echoing sound of locking cogs, followed by humming. It sounded as though the alien machinery was clanking into new modes of pursuit. A dark shadow passed over the green, sunlit foliage. In the new gloomy surroundings, the loud whirring of the fighting machine's hydraulics continued. A sinister immobility gripped all. What next? How would it come? When?

Everyone was frozen with fear as the giant shadow above the trees made a long, deep, lingering call.

Aloo-ugh!

It was like an angry cow, its call magnified a thousand times. The booming resonance shook the earth and trees, causing everything and everyone to shake with terror. The petrified group of people could not see the machine's capsule, in which sat the vengeful alien intent upon killing. Yet they imagined the giant trunk with its big, green, orbed spy window. Was the Martian trying to peer through the leafy foliage in search of them?

Reg clutched at his shotgun as he lay on his stomach. Lewis sat with his back pressed firmly against a tree trunk while clasping his shotgun faithfully. Both French sailors held their rifles in readiness, yet all knew their weapons would be useless against the machine.

A short way off, came the sound of a flaying whip. As each person turned to focus on the strange sound, they perceived a flaying tentacle. It descended from the leafy foliage. The erratic thrashing stopped and the sensitive tentacle feeler went to ground. It slinked off like a snake searching in the wrong direction. It had moved away from the group.

Another flaying feeler dropped to the other side of them. It settled for a moment, then slithered away towards the western fringe. Then a third fell amid the group. Everyone rolled away avoiding the thrashing sensor. Then each froze in a new position, too terrified to make a run. The strange component slithered like a worm over the hard mud of the wood's floor. It was like a giant metal rat's tail, which made them all shiver with revulsion. Each person was forced to remain still and watch the hideous feeler manoeuvring with nimbleness and disgusting grace.

Lewis froze as the feeler ran its touch over the tree trunk where he was hiding. He watched, wide-eyed with fear, as the cold-looking tail end of the sensor lingered before his sweating face. His eyes closed and he gulped, while all around held their breath. If the thing recognised him it would lasso

The Last Days of the Fighting Machine

him in a split second and wrench him up through the trees.

Mrs Steed felt terrified for him, reliving the experience of being dragged through the bedroom window of her cottage and held high in the sky before being unceremoniously slung into a cage at the fighting machine's back.

In her soul she prayed that it would not happen to Lewis Puttnam. He did not deserve to die in such a way. He was always the infallible rogue who could get out of anything.

As though in answer to her prayers the sensor turned away, slithering towards a bush where one of the French sailors was hiding. The young man remained still, but Gippy wrinkled her snout and snapped at the feeler.

The tentacle became a quick lashing blur as it instantly looped around the wretched yapping terrier and caught it. It did not retreat up through the foliage with its prey but lingered as though tormenting. The wretched little terrier squealed and yelped for help but none dared. Bisset who had saved her earlier looked on helpless, but adamant he would not make such a mistake a second time. All watched as the doomed little dog was slowly dragged across the earth squealing and thrashing in a futile attempt to wriggle free. Then, as though the Martian controlling the artificial limb knew his tantalising bait would not produce a human rescuer, the tentacle rose up through the foliage with Gippy's sorrowful howling echoing through dark shadowed foliage.

"We should move," said Mrs Steed. "It found the dog here and it might reason that there are more of us."

Lewis raised himself and looked to the two French sailors and whispered. "Find somewhere else to hide."

They seemed to understand him and nodded as each stood and moved towards new areas cover.

"Be careful, Reg," said his mother as she held Jimmy's hand. "There are other tentacles, remember."

"Yes, Mum," he replied in an infantile manner, but still clasped the shotgun in one hand. The other clutched the scythe. They all rose and crept through the trees and bushes, which were much darker now the tripod was standing over the woodland. Above, its engines were rolling like a giant factory hovering ominously above them. It was searching for people, and reluctant to leave until it found them.

Suddenly, on to one side of the fugitive group, another flaying tentacle dropped like hissing a snake in the Garden of Eden. The appendages stopped and bounced angrily short of the floor. It hovered with a strange lens in a square box at the end. Almost like a camera.

The hunted people went to ground, crawling behind bushes, tree trunks and dips in the muddy floor. Anything that offered protection. They were being hunted and all were at their wits end. How could they get out of the terrifying dilemma?

"ALOOOOUGHH!"

Again, the deep, booming deep sound tore down through the darkened woodland. It was clear the Martian in its machine was continuing with its search.

Two more tentacles dropped down through the leafy canopy. They slowed their descent and calmly lowered the last part of the way to the woodland floor. Two immediately slithered towards the group. Probing and prodding dips and bushes, in a search for human flesh. One began to slither along the bark of a tree where Laurent was. The French sailor took a slow and cautious step away from the tree before electing to remain still. The alien feeler began to explore the tree as it wound around the entire trunk. For a moment it seemed Laurent had made a good decision.

A high-pitched whipping sound screamed out through the wood like a speeding blur. One moment Laurent was standing there like a statue. Then he was entwined by the second speeding sensor. The quick whiplash had him with decisive speed.

Laurent screamed out as the feeler upon the tree leapt out and secured him more firmly. The wretched man had no time to struggle as he shot up through the foliage like a rocket. One moment he was standing there, and in the next instant he was gone.

Lewis turned to the Bisset, the young man who had tried to save little Gippy. The young man was cursing with tears in his eyes. "Oh Mon Dieu! Ils ont pris Laurent."

Suddenly the shadow lifted as the trunk rose higher above the wood. They heard the Martian vehicle's feet rising as the fighting machine stepped back over the woods. It had gone back to the wide mud track leading back into Paglesham Churchend.

"It's leaving," said Lewis.

"Why has it stopped now?" asked Mrs Steed.

The inclination suddenly dawned across Lewis's face. "It only saw a dog and one of the seamen who rescued it. The Martian has one dog and one seaman. I don't think it knows we are here."

The thunderous steps shook the ground, but it was no more than a shuffle past the poplar trees and cottages back to the burning church. They all scurried through the woods towards the fringe that looked out down the mud track into the village. They crept to the very eastern corner of the trees by the beginning of a field hedge wall. It offered them a view through the smashed poplar trees at the burning church. The machine was standing above the flaming ruin like a giant demonic sentinel. The old church tower was intact, but the other part was now burning wreckage. Tall flames licked the air as the fires continued to burn robustly.

"The side of your cottage is on fire, Mrs Steed," said Lewis.

She nodded and through her unkempt matted hair and dirty face, she replied. "Right now, I think that is the least of anyone's worries."

A human scream rang out from the blue sky above. All looked up to see the wiggling form of Laurent. The French sailor was held before the fighting machine's green luminous porthole by one of the appendages.

"Oh my God!" muttered Mrs Steed. "Jimmy, come with me back into the woods. You too, Reggie." Her grandson and son submitted to her demand and went into the wood. Lewis and Bisset were compelled to watch on in horror.

"The bastard is tormenting the poor man," muttered Lewis through gritted teeth. He shook his head and locked his jaw defiantly. "I'd love to bring that thing down."

Bisset said nothing, but forced himself to watch as more flaying tentacles hovered before the screaming man.

"Que fait-on?" Bisset asked.

"Oh, my God!" whispered Lewis as it began to dawn. He had seen the Martians perform such callous acts before. He saw the thick barb on the end of one of the appendages. His heart sank as the helpless cries of Laurent continued. Lewis took a deep breath and resigned himself. He watched as the long hypodermic spine plunged into Laurent's kicking body. It pierced the soft part where his shoulder connected to his neck.

Laurent's high-pitched scream rose several notches then abruptly stopped. He began to convulse as an alien enzyme was pumped into his body. The intense seizure was horrendous, and the wretched man vomited green foaming bile. His spasmodic shaking became more violent as his head and legs kicked and thrashed wildly. Suddenly, his agonised death throes stopped. Laurent just hung there in a state of helpless paralysis. A second cruel curved barb came down at the end of another feeler. It punctured the other side of his neck and shoulder connection. Instantly, the device began to suck Laurent's body clean of blood. His mouth fell open and his eye lids raised to reveal the blood-shot whites of his eyeballs. No irises could be seen. They were raised upwards as though by the suction, beyond the upper eye lid. Looking up into his head. Out of sight into his vanquished mind.

Sucked clean of his blood, the dead form of Laurent was cast into the burning ruins of the church.

"Let's get back into the woods," Lewis gripped Bisset's shoulder. "Come on mate, let's get away from here." He was almost imploring with the young man, who finally and reluctantly nodded his acceptance. They retreated back into the woods.

As they left, the agonised screams of Laurent were still echoing in each man's head. A shocking memory echoing in his mind. Lewis had seen it happen before. It remained as wicked and horrific as the first time. Bisset was deeply disturbed by the evil. It was the youngster's first time of witnessing the Martians' feeding. Drinking people through a straw while they were still alive and paralysed. The Martians' were as indifferent to people as people were to sheep or poultry. The invaders had turned Britain into an abattoir. A human slaughterhouse.

They came upon Mrs Steed and her family. "I know what they have done to the poor man," she said. "We watched it happen to Mrs Walker."

Lewis sighed despondently. "They got Mrs Walker?" He remembered the publican's wife. A stern and often reproachful lady.

"What can we do?" whispered Mrs Steed as she clutched her grandson, terrified that the fighting machine might do the same to her offspring. For a moment she looked at the single-barrelled shotgun clutched in her free hand. She entertained the thought of ending it all quickly. What hope could there be? What hope for mankind?

"We're not dead yet, Mrs Steed, and I don't intend going without a fight. Plus, the bastards are dying." Lewis was frightened but angry and he chose to bathe in the ferocity that pulsated through his veins, allowing the fear to moderate and stop him from acting rashly. "The others are coming and they will have the small cannon. If we could just get close enough to have a clear shot at the trunk, that machine could be damaged beyond repair. The *Thunder Child* did it at Maldon. I witnessed it from the shoreline. It can happen again."

Reg was shaking with fear, and asked. "What can we do, Lewis? They might not get here quick enough."

"They will, Reggie, and in the meantime, we stay here and keep watch. That thing does not know we are here."

"It knows about us," added Jimmy. "We got Granny from the machine's cage when it was standing by the church tower. There were two of them. They went into the church. Uncle Reg shot one up as it tried to crawl away."

Lewis looked at Reg. It had not escaped his notice that the mentally challenged Reg was covered in dust and layers of blood. But so was Mrs Steed. Yet Reg was smothered from head to foot. Lewis was shocked and in awe. "You got one of the bastards Reg?" He had a look of elation. "How did you manage that?"

"The machine was left empty. The two Martians went into the bell tower. They left the machine unattended," answered Mrs Steed and then hissed triumphantly. "One messed with my Reggie and got more then it bargained for."

The simple man held up his shotgun with a look of gleeful malice.

"Tell me about it all, and don't miss out anything."

They huddled together in the woods and enjoyed the tale of Mrs Steed's rescue and Reg's killing of a Martian. Fearful, they could delight in the tale of Reg's revenge. It passed the time waiting for P.C. Llewellyn and the rest of the French Navy crew. All were blindly confident in the local policeman. He would turn up soon with the rest of the sailors and their artillery piece.

CHAPTER 8

PRIMING THE FIELD GUN

It had been a full twenty minutes since Blanc and Llewellyn had retreated to the base of the hedgerow with the four other seamen. The explosion from Paglesham Churchend had forced them to abandon the artillery piece on the mud flats. All had been listening to Blanc's commentary on the events of the tripod, as it straddled the distant woodland and lowered its tentacles through the leafy roof and pulled out the unfortunate Laurent.

"My God, are you sure it did that, Mister Blanc." Llewellyn was outraged by the account.

"I am positive, Policeman Llewellyn. It sucked blood from one of my men and then threw him into the flames of the old church."

Llewellyn's nostrils flared. "It devoured the poor man alive! Why would it be so malicious? These things kill without remorse. It is as though they are angry with us. They are dying from something and perhaps they blame us. I always thought the brutes were devoid of any form of feeling."

"I don't think it is anger, Policeman Llewellyn. I think they kill merely to feed from our blood. They are as indifferent to us as we are to sheep or cows. We are nothing to them."

"Well, these fiends must know we are prepared to fight by now. A few of them have gone down to human fury. But most are just getting ill and dying." Llewellyn took his helmet off and wiped the sweat from his forehead with a handkerchief.

"Your poacher friend and Bisset must still be in the wood." Blanc's huge moustache and beard wriggled beneath his nose. He bit his lip nervously. "We will go back for the gun and continue. I am sure we can get the artillery piece along the bank and out of view of this Martian. If the machine stays there, we can get a close-range shot at the thing. Perhaps the Martian is complacent – oui? "

Llewellyn put his helmet back on. "There is a stepping stile further up. It comes out by the church grounds. We'll be almost beneath the machine. But firing at the confounded thing and missing barely defies thought. The machine will be on us, Mr Blanc. We will be for the same fate as your poor crewman."

"Then we must not miss. And when we hit, we must scatter in different directions."

Llewellyn undid the top button of his tunic. It was hot and he felt uncomfortable. He took a deep breath and closed his eyes before replying.

"Right, boyo, let's get to it then." He rose, walked back onto the bank and stood by one of the wheels of the field gun. "Let's do it now. I don't want to think about it too much. I just want to get on with it, you see."

Blanc smiled and looked to his men. "Passer ensuite," he muttered as he stood up and followed Llewellyn to the field gun. Four subordinate crewmen looked to one another with concerned expressions, then reluctantly followed. Within moments, all were rolling the gun along the bank as quickly and stealthily as their condition allowed.

As they got closer along the embankment, they could see the empty boat hangers of another boat yard. There was also the smell of burning from the old church, along with the sound of crackling embers. The breeze made each man's nostrils flare. They hugged the lower scarp of the rise, knowing that the lone machine was by the burning wreckage. Only the rise and the tall hedgerow would shield them from view.

Llewellyn was sweating from their toil, and his anxious eyes kept peering up at the top of the rise as though expecting that the machine to loom into view against the drifting smoke and the clear blue sky.

"Only weeks ago, that fire would have brought several more of the things over," he muttered to Blanc. "But now we expect to move around without the others interfering. There must be something wrong. It must be gravely bad for the Martians. The fire is not attracting more of them."

"Yes," Blanc shook his head. "The others must be able to see the smoke, but for some reason there is no interest and no more machines in sight. Perhaps they are too ill to come here, or the matter is no longer important to them. I wonder what made this particular machine come here alone. It seems uncharacteristic of this one, when the rest are trying to go south. I would think that more of them must be dying and the process might be speeding up."

"I know that this one had a blast hole in its side. Yet it can still move about, as we have just observed."

Blanc frowned. "However, this machine seems reluctant to leave the vicinity. As you have said. Maybe it can't travel too far?"

As the group came closer to the boatyard hangers, they came across a small pathway cut into the rise towards the tall hedgerow. At the end, the stile was in sight. From beyond the hedge, the burning church could be heard. About them were scattered stones from the destruction of the church. They reached the stile, and moved the field gun into position.

The old house of worship was gone, apart from the belfry. Each man's angle of vision just took in the top of the fighting machine's trunk. They were hidden behind the hedgerow. The machine was motionless, looking out over the burning debris with its back to the tall hedgerow. It seemed to be observing the woodlands beyond the line of poplar trees, unaware of the new group and their artillery gun behind.

"We'll need to be as quiet as possible," whispered Llewellyn nervously. He wanted to say that he was unsure about what they were about to attempt, but thought better of it. The French sailors seemed resolved to make the attempt, now that they had come so far.

As the band of men set the small cannon up, it seemed as though they were making an awful noise. Fortunately, the burning wreckage of the church had drowned out their approach. By the stile, they elevated the cannon's barrel over the fence post. The dreadful and magnificent sight of the Martian machine loomed before them – a colossal edifice towering into the smoke-filled sky, a demented and horrific sentinel over the devastation of stone and flame. It appeared completely unaware of the human presence approaching from behind. The machine's attention remained focused on the woodland beyond the road leading out of the village. At such close range, the tiny beings behind could not miss the exposed casing of the machine, which contained the Martian beings.

Blanc whispered instructions in French, and his men stealthily went about the task of loading the breach with a shell and then elevating the gun barrel at an acute angle of about eighty degrees. The trajectory was perfect at such close range. The high body trunk that rested upon the tripod limbs was clearly in sight.

Each man felt the sweat of fear. The machine might become mobile and move away from the gun sights, ruining the line of fire they were meticulously preparing. One clear shot was all they would have. All knew, this shot needed to count.

Blanc whispered instructions in French. Then he turned to Llewellyn and repeated in English. "There might not be a chance of a second shot. We must try to escape upon firing. We must try not to group or we will all get caught."

"How are we going to know which paths to take?" Llewellyn was anxious. All hell was about to break loose. It would be every man for himself. "We should all try to make for the woods, where Lewis and your other man are. Perhaps Mrs Steed's family too."

"You must lead the escape before we fire the cannon. In fact, I want all of you to leave now. It will only take one to fire." He looked around at his men. Then began to explain in French that he wanted them to leave, while he remained alone to fire the shell.

Llewellyn implored to Blanc. "We must get past the wall right under the thing. Move towards the first house and along the terrace cottages. Then across the road to the little wood opposite the other end of the village. Tell your men to follow me."

The old quartermaster smiled and nodded his head before relaying the policeman's instructions in French. The sailors nodded their compliance reluctantly, and lined up behind Llewellyn. He climbed through the wooden posts of the stile rather than step over it. Each man copied him, and all nimbly made their way along the old stone wall of the church grounds towards the first of the terraced cottages.

Blanc looked on as his men made their way past the derelict homes. They reached the first cottage and pushed further along to the other end of the terrace, by an old public house and an overturned horse cart. He was content as they sped across the pathway and passed the broken row of poplar trees, disappearing into the small woodlands and out of sight.

Blanc sighed. It was now all down to him and he felt a little more at ease knowing his men were out of the way. He looked up through the drifting black smoke towards the soaring alien body trunk silhouetted against the blue sky. He swallowed. It was the time to act. Everything was primed, and he once more checked the cannon's sights. The fighting machine's trunk was snug within the gun's trajectory. With gritted teeth he firmly grabbed the firing mechanism. One, two, three – he sharply yanked the lever.

There was a boom as the artillery piece jolted and fire leapt from the barrel. The wicked shell ripped into the underbelly of the Martian machine. It instantly erupted in a roaring ball of flame and smoke. A high-pitched and unearthly scream emitted from the alien amplifier system. The huge legs staggered sideways, trying pathetically to get away from the blazing wreckage beneath its carriage and between its mechanical limbs. More high-pitched panic and agonised screams emitted from the machine's peculiar mega-hailer, the very device used to boom out the Martian battle cry.

With thunderous and unsteady gigantic steps, the flaming machine lumbered – twisting around as though trying to chase its tail of fire. Each huge step crashing into the Earth. Turning towards the stile in a state of burning despair, the huge contraption took another giant step forward. Shrill, agonised screams were still emitting from the hailer device. Inside the capsule, the Martian must have been suffering extensively. The gigantic machine lifted a huge leg over the tall hedgerow and the stile where the artillery piece was. The gun's guilty barrel still smoking. The Martian inside took no notice of the instrument. The vehicle was piloted towards the river inlet. The flaming upper body trunk passed over the stile and gun, the colossal leg carrying the burning machine away from the area – towards the old boat yard like a demented and screaming crab.

Blanc had thrown himself into the long red weeds for cover. He watched as the burning machine passed, staring up in awe as the huge flaming underbelly travelled over. It was belching out fire and smoke, blocking out the blue sky. Angry tentacles were whipping about the enormous monstrosity, flaying and hissing wildly, slapping and whipping the burning body trunk.

As some of the appendages erratically started whipping beneath the trunk, the action caused Blanc to flinch in fear. He thought the feelers were going to scoop him up. Thankfully, he was wrong. The thrashing limbs were trying to put out the stricken machine's flames.

The tripod fighting machine moved on with giant strides out onto the mud flats and shallow river inlet, where it stopped. A huge pipe emerged from the machine into the shallow river and began to suck up water. Spraying sea water was released from the tentacles beneath the machine's burning underbelly. Soon the limbs were spraying the flames from many directions.

Blanc looked on spellbound as the machine tended itself. It screamed out defiantly as another spinal cord, with a funnelled apparatus at the end, rose above the burning trunk. A whirling flame spiralled within the hollow and then a glowing ray shout out and combed the hedge and dyke in a line of sweeping flame. Blanc was forced to bury himself in a ditch. The heat was intense and he almost broke cover. He only managed to restrain himself by crawling frantically along the ditch between the dyke and flaming hedgerow. Fortune had favoured him – only the rise of the dyke had protected him from intensity of the heat ray. He was gathering his frightened wits and he began to reason that the Martian did not know where the attack had come from. That was why the machine had combed the area with its heat ray. Blanc's acute mind began to click into reason, and his heart skipped a beat. He saw the artillery piece intact, with flames blazing either side of it. Somehow the stile had been protected by the rise of the dyke and the angle from which the heat ray had come. His eyes blazed when he saw the shells close by and the blazing flames a little way off. He leapt forwards and dragged the box away. Sliding the shells down into the ditch and away from the burning hedge. The gun! If only he could move the gun. He might get a second shot.

Aloo-Ugh!

From beyond the rise of the dyke came the screech of the machine. It seemed filled with rage. The Martian inside would still be injured, despite the flames having now been extinguished.

It was of no avail to Blanc. His adrenalin was racing and his blood lust was up. He could get another shot at the brute in its huge fighting machine. One more shot. If he could move fast enough.

Leaping upon the gun, he frantically tried to turn the field piece. Gradually, amid the crackle of the burning hedgerow, he managed the feat. The barrel was now pointing towards the mud flats, where the giant fighting machine still tended its hissing and smouldering damage. A second shot would be awkward, but not unattainable. The field piece was light but could pack a punch at close range. Slowly he began to roll the field piece forward. He stopped just before the path that cut through the dyke rose out onto the mud flats. The rise still hid him from the view of the stricken machine. Behind him on either side, the inferno bathed him in heat. He knew it would be better to load the field piece straight away. He would not be able to waste time doing this once he wheeled the gun further forward to aim at his target.

Blanc went back and jumped down into the ditch. Quickly, he grabbed a second shell before returning to the gun and opening the breech. Fear and excitement caused his hands to tremble. He wondered how long it might be before the flame and damage had abated sufficiently for the machine to attack. The thought of repair caused him to sweat. A cold stroke of fear in such heat. It lightly swept down his spine. His mouth was dry and he licked his lips, taking a deep breath before summoning up one last handful of courage. Then gulping it down into a determined resolve, he pushed the artillery piece forward along the mud path. The gun nestled neatly before the dyke's cutting.

The machine was still there. It was towering high upon its three limbs, standing in the mud flats and still spraying the flame beneath its smoking under body. Rising steam hissed up and about its damaged capsule. The hazy cloud lingered before the small compound green port hole. Blanc reasoned that the Martian's vision would be impaired by the steam. It was a valuable moment for Blanc. He knew he had seconds to take advantage of the situation. Allowing the spent shell casing to fall out of the open breech, Blanc replaced with the new shell and locked the wicked projectile in place. Once again, he carefully lined up the gun. Taking care to lower the elevation the barrel. Fitting the smoking machine's trunk firmly within the gun sights. The shot would not be as point-blank as the first. Yet it was still at a distance that was easy enough for an artilleryman to strike. Quartermaster Blanc was used to firing the huge breech loading guns of F.S. *Ney*. This small artillery piece was, in some ways, familiar to him.

Blanc indulged himself with a malicious grin. His bushy beard and moustache moving with the contours of his smiling and sweating face. Once again, he grabbed the firing lever. He yanked the mechanism and the artillery piece leapt back from the kick. It spat out more angry flame with a muffled boom. The shell propelled its way over shingle and mud flaps into the colossal machine's upper trunk. It ripped through the rising steam and into the fighting machine's curved forehead, just above the concave green orb. The explosion was one of glorious destruction for Blanc's gleeful eyes to feast upon. He watched the machine wither again against the violent impact. The tripod struggled to stay standing amid another rising orange ball of expanding flame. The colossal alien apparatus staggered as the creature inside battled to maintain control. Via the alien megaphone, the torment of the Martian inside could be clearly heard – a high-pitched, unearthly wailing that spread across the landscape.

Blanc turned and fled towards the stile, which had blazing foliage on either side. Leaping upon the step and nimbly over the fixed gateway onto a pathway, he ran along the perimeter of Paglesham Churchend's destroyed and burning church. He ran for all his worth along the cottage terraces and the line of smashed poplar trees. He tripped and fell, sprawling amid the broken roof slates and glass that littered the roadway. He was cursing as he rose, cut and grazed from the debris about him.

From beyond the smashed poplar trees before the little woodland began, he heard the desperate pleas of his men imploring him to keep running.

Aloo ugh!

The roar was deafening. Blanc turned and looked up. Against the smoke-filled summer sky, he perceived the flaming monster stepping over the burning hedgerow. A vast course of black smoke spread in its wake. A thunderous step crashed down on the village roadway, another high-pitched shriek bellowed out of the speaker system. One more step and it would be in the village and upon the desperately fleeing quartermaster. The Martian inside still had control of the machine, though it was obviously a struggle. Yet it was still being piloted towards

Blanc. The ground shook as another giant step hit the dirt road.

Blanc realised he would not make the woodlands. He elected to clamber through one of the missing windows of a terraced cottage. Scrambling through an opening, he fell onto the floor of a wrecked front room. At the same moment, the heat ray tore through the wall above him and into the wall opposite. Flame and debris cascaded about the room as Blanc curled into a ball. The proximity of the heat ray was too close for comfort. He felt as though he was being slow cooked. Frantically, he crawled upon his belly, desperate to be away from the window. He crawled towards the lounge door, where fire was licking the wall. The growing heat was becoming overpowering. Soon it would be too much to bear, and he would have to get out. Outside he could hear the Martian heat ray firing again. It was further along the terraced block. The alien was systematically incinerating the entire block of cottages. Blanc twisted and turned, frantically patting hot dust and soot from his head. He was caught in the annihilation, and realised the concentrated spread of the heat ray was for him alone.

The entire building was collapsing. Joists and plaster dropped through the flames. He was choking in the dust, and tried to cover his mouth. A huge beam and lump of plaster fell across him.

The flat section of debris protected him like a giant shield as more tumbling rubble fell about the room. Squeezing his eyes firmly shut and covering his mouth and nostrils, he decided that this was as good a hiding place as he was likely to find for the moment.

Outside, thick black smoke continued to billow from various parts of the fighting machine. Grey swirls streamed out. Then it staggered, and the heat ray ceased. It reeled backwards towards the end of the collapsed cottages. The Martian must have been battling frantically to keep the machine upright. Its giant foot boomed down upon the earth. Another steadying step. The machine appeared to gain composure, then took another stride back onto the rise of the old graveyard. It returned to the wrecked and burning church, stopping next to the belfry tower.

Dubois and Lefebvre left the others in the wood as they emerged with rifles raised. Each man feared for Blanc in the burning house. They moved around the smashed poplar trees and took aim at the giant machine and opened fire. It was a foolhardy thing to do, but the brave sailors desperately needed to distract the Martian, at least long enough to allow their quartermaster to escape from the burning building. Bullets pinged harmlessly against the fighting machine's elevated smouldering trunk.

The machine's joints groaned, and it tilted. The silhouette inside was peering out through the green orb. The Martian perceived the tiny beings were defiantly trying to inflict further harm. These humans had already caused severe pain. For a moment, the alien creature lingered. Perhaps it was wondering how two of the first hits had ruptured its body armour, while the other attacks had been puny. Perhaps it pondered many things, before making a decision.

A spine tentacle lifted above the body trunk. It held the apparatus that fired the heat ray. The Martian must have decided further speculation was unproductive. There was a glow within the funnelled apparatus, which tilted down. The heat ray shot out as Dubois and Lefebvre were instantly consumed into a ball of flame. The surrounding broken tree foliage erupted too. There was no scream of pain, the sailors knew nothing. Flesh was devoured in a fraction of a second. Charred and smouldering skeletons dropped to the ground.

From the sanctuary of the woodlands, Mrs Steed put her hands to her mouth in order to prevent herself from screaming in terror. The other sailors were cursing in their own language. Lewis and P.C. Llewellyn tried to restrain the angry Bisset, fearing he might make the same rash mistake as Dubois and Lefebvre.

The Last Days of the Fighting Machine

"Look!" called young Jimmy excitedly, pointing at the Martian tripod. "The thing is staggering again. I think it's going to fall."

One of its legs slowly buckled. The colossal machine eased down on a knee-type joint. Another thunderous crash shook the earth. Machine appendages flayed out from various parts of the smoking body trunk. They tried to wrap securely about the ruined church tower. Harshly, amid the creaking groans of its huge joints, the machine eased, then slid down the stone wall of the tower. Finally, it settled, lying against the base of the belfry. The body trunk was smashed and punctured by shell hits. Smoke and dust billowed about as the tentacles released their grip and retracted into the giant machine. They lay still and hissing. Thick grey swirls of fog spewed from joints, drifting up into the clear blue sky. Crackling fires were burning all about from the destruction of the church in a bizarre landscape of green and pink patchwork vegetation.

Two more of the French sailors, Linville and Segal, crept across the pathway. They moved around the poplar trees towards the burning skeletal remains of their shipmates. They aimed their rifles in readiness, but must have surely known that they would be useless against the machine. However, the structure did not seem to be working anymore. The giant machine had collapsed and was wrecked.

P.C. Llewellyn looked towards the last French sailor Bisset, the young man who had tried to save Gippy.

"Bisset?" Llewellyn said, and the young sailor turned to him. "You stay here, understand." The policeman pointed at the youngster and at the ground about them. He then pointed at Linville and Segal as they crept out towards the burning church grounds. He shook his head indicating that it was not a good thing to do.

Bisset nodded his head with reluctant compliance, realising what the British policeman was trying to tell him.

"I don't believe it," Lewis hissed excitedly. "The blooming thing has gone down! The quartermaster did that! God bless him."

"Mr Blanc is still in that cottage over there. We must get to him." Llewellyn began to move forward, but Mrs Steed held his arm.

"No, wait P.C. Llewellyn, we can't go yet," she implored. "I can't believe that no other machines have come. Look at the fire and smoke. It's bound to attract more."

"It will not happen any longer, Mrs Steed." replied Lewis. "They would have come by now. The Martians are dying in swarms. Their machines are just stopping to die. There are barely any left now. There is something wrong with them. There are fewer each passing day. We all know that now. We must search the cottage that Blanc went into. He might still be alive."

Llewellyn looked at Mrs Steed. "You stay here with your lads. We'll go and search." He looked to Bisset and said: "Come on lad, I'm sure you will want to find Quartermaster Blanc."

There was a nod of approval and the smiling seaman made off with the policeman and the poacher.

Jimmy was about to follow, but his grandmother reached for him and scolded. "Oh no you don't, young man. You stay here with Reg and me."

"But Gran…" he implored.

"No buts, young man, you stay here," she reprimanded firmly.

Llewellyn, Lewis and Bisset moved cautiously towards the burning cottages. Around the other side of the smashed poplar trees and towards the very window they had seen Blanc scamper inside just before the heat ray ripped into it. The slicing malevolence of fire had torn through the length of the entire terrace. The upper parts and the roof beams of the whole block had collapsed into the ground floors, making the cottages look like derelict bungalows. There were scattered fires everywhere. More billowing smoke was rising, blocking out the daylight. The mangled array of the village poplar trees was beginning to burn too. The broken branches and scattered bracken needed little encouragement.

Bisset was speaking to himself in French in tones of panic and concern. Llewellyn tried to calm the anxious young man.

"We'll find him, lad. Don't do anything rash now, please. Try to remain calm." Llewellyn used his hands to signify calm. Bisset comprehended, and ceased his morbid muttering.

Lewis looked through the window and was instantly downhearted. Bricks, wooden beams and floor boards. All piled up where the floor should have been. He sighed. Hope for Blanc began to fade. No man could have got out of such destruction alive. The lower walls acted like a gigantic bin that contained the collapsed rubble of the upper part of the dwellings. He climbed upon the window seal to be confronted by a wall of debris.

"Mister Blanc," he called. "Mister Blanc, can you hear me?"

About the three men, scattered fires blazed – from the church, the branches of the poplar trees and the long, high hedgerow that cut the village off from the approach to the creek. Everywhere was bathed in flame and ruin. The pretty little village was unrecognisable. However, the devastation was locked out of each man's perception. They were totally occupied with concern for Quartermaster Blanc.

"Mr Blanc," called Llewellyn, adding his own contribution to Lewis' call. "Can you hear us? Give us a sign, anything!"

A muffled call came from the rubble before them, and all suddenly came alive with hope and excitement. Lewis and Llewellyn climbed into the wrecked building.

"It came from under that beam." Lewis started to cough as the dust began to get into his throat.

Llewellyn sneezed also feeling the effects of the thick dust. "Are you sure?"

"Positive," he coughed. "Get young Bisset to help us." He began to splutter as he pulled out a dirty handkerchief to cover his nose and mouth. "Cover your mouth. This dust is very thick and will take some time to settle."

Llewellyn complied and beckoned to Bisset. Wanting the youngster to enter, while pointing to his covered face, instructing him to do likewise. Bisset understood the crude hand signs. He acted in accordance with the advice, scrambling through the window. Together, Llewellyn and Bisset stepped gingerly upon the rubble. They made towards the beam where Lewis was waiting for help. Soon there were three of them ready to raise the beam.

"One, two, three, heave!" ordered Llewellyn.

All strained and lifted the beam. It moved a little easier than expected.

"Bisset," Llewellyn said. "Take a look."

The youngster spoke no English but knew what was being asked. He obeyed, and gave a call of delight. "Il est là."

Bisset reached beneath the boarding and pulled Blanc out from the smashed plaster, and bricks. The beam was let go once the Frenchman was free.

"Well, Mr Blanc, I am pleased to see you," added Llewellyn.

"Thank you, Policeman Llewellyn," replied Blanc, starting to cough. All assisted Quartermaster Blanc towards the window. He was covered in dust. His huge black beard and moustache were grey from the soot. He continued coughing convulsively.

Outside, Mrs Steed, Reg and Jimmy watched from the perimeter of the wood.

"They have all climbed in," said Mrs Steed, pushing back the bedraggled, dust-filled hair from her face. Congealed blood was still crusting the side of her head.

"The Frenchmen's leader must be in there," said Jimmy. "He jumped through that window after running from the fighting machine."

"Should we help them, Mum?" Reg wanted to be in the village with the rest.

"No," she replied. "But we will work our way out along the field. I want to see if that thing is dead."

The Last Days of the Fighting Machine

They looked at the smouldering poplar trees, the cottages and the church. There were scattered fires everywhere.

"The flames are not spreading," said Reg.

"No, they are not," agreed his mother. "They were abating."

"Will the burning stop?" asked Jimmy. He looked over to the tall hedgerow that ran parallel with the river inlet. "The red weed is burning too."

"The red weed will be all gone – soon," replied Reg.

"Come on now, boys. Follow me." Mrs Steed cautiously led the way out into the field, crouching as they went forward, using the stone wall for cover. When they were opposite the church, Mrs Steed chanced to peep over the wall. She observed the gigantic form of the fallen fighting machine laying across the devastated church debris, with its body trunk resting upon the bell tower's wall.

"That's a sight for sore eyes," she muttered with an air of satisfaction.

"Our house is nearly gone," said Reg indignantly. "Where are we going to live?"

"There must be a large number of vacant properties, Reggie. Right now, that's not important." Mrs Steed turned her attention back to the wrecked cottages. She was delighted to see the bearded Frenchman, who she had last seen fleeing the fighting machine. He emerged with Bisset. Lewis and P.C. Llewellyn were following.

Mrs Steed looked at Reg and Jimmy. "That is the quartermaster who Lewis and Llewellyn had been telling us about, covered in dust, cuts and bruises. He is the man responsible for bringing down a tripod."

Her son and grandson were instantly at the wall beside her, eager to watch what was developing.

"Is that Blanc?" asked Jimmy.

"It is," answered his grandmother with an air of gratitude for the brave and industrious man.

"Uncle Reg killed a Martian too," added Jimmy.

Mrs Steed smiled at her two boys. Son and grandson. "He did too, Jimmy. You showed that Martian what was what didn't you, Reggie."

Reg grinned sheepishly. But he barely had time to savour the compliment. His face became concerned as he stared towards the burning churchyard, where the fighting machine lay.

"The tube that fires the heat ray is moving!" He pointed at it.

"Get down!" yelled Mrs Steed. She grabbed Reg and Jimmy. They fell flat to the grass behind the stone wall. The whirring sound of the heat ray's funnel could be heard before the beam screeched out. Further along, a section of the wall erupted as the heat rays smashed through it. Then the concentrated beam sliced along the entire stone partition. Boulders exploded and scattered in all directions. Mrs Steed and her family huddled into a protective ball as the stone works fell upon and about them. The heat ray stopped just before the moving, white-hot beam was upon their section of the wall.

"Crawl away," Mrs Steed commanded. "Back to the woods."

"We should have stayed there," said Jimmy. "Why did we come out here?"

"I wanted to see if the machine was dead. From a distance. I'm glad we did. What happened to the two sailors who went to investigate?" Mrs Steed had suddenly thought of the two men who had advanced earlier with guns raised.

By the cottage, Llewellyn had called out in alarm. They had all watched the heat ray ripping along the stone wall.

"The bloody thing is still firing its heat ray, able to fire from the crashed position. It's lying there unable to walk but still firing." Lewis was angry and amazed at the same time.

The sound of whirring was heard again. The fighting machine's weapon was pressuring up again. Llewellyn called Bisset and the quartermaster back to the wall. "It can't see us from here."

As the whirring stopped the heat ray shot out. It cut through the last bedraggled line of the already burning poplar trees. A line of blazing light sliced through each trunk like a hot knife through a block of butter. They watched in awe as the first few trees fell like giant skittles.

Then the heat ray suddenly switched off. It had stopped halfway along the tree line. Yet the spectacle of those tall trees already spliced played out. One by one, four of the beautiful trees fell amid creaking protests, smashing across the dirt track and into onto the already felled block of cottages.

Lewis ran towards the fallen tree trunks. He looked carefully towards the church grounds, keeping the wrecked cottages between himself and the view from the churchyard. The crippled machine was lying over the graveyard with its body trunk against the base of the belfry tower. Yet it was still able to use its heat ray.

"What does it take to kill these bloody things?" he cursed.

"What are you doing, Lewis?" Llewellyn called from the cover of the cottages.

"Mrs Steed and the boys went out into the field. I saw them from the window." He pressed on, using the collapsed tree foliage as cover as he scrambled over the wrecked field wall.

"Get down, Mr Puttnam," called Mrs Steed. She was lying on her stomach, with Reg and Jimmy by the woodland fringe. "That thing is still up for the fight."

Lewis dropped on to his stomach. "Are you all right, Mrs Steed? Are the boys all right?"

"Yes," all three replied in unison. They were singed and battered, their faces reddened, burned from being in close proximity to the heat ray.

"Can you move towards me?" he asked. "We must get back to the cover of the cottages."

Mrs Steed scampered through the foliage, pulling Jimmy with her, while Reg followed. When they reached Lewis, all stopped and took a breather.

Mrs Steed pushed her dusty and matted hair over her blood streaked scalp. "I'm not sure about this, Mr Puttnam. The woods seemed a better idea."

Reg added his support. "The machine is still firing. It will get us as we try to cross the road."

"We should be all right," added Lewis. "The fallen trees will offer us a lot of cover, and only a part of the road is within the machine's view."

"That's not so reassuring, Mr Puttnam," answered Mrs Steed nervously.

"If we can get back, you'll have better cover than you've got here."

"What about the wood." She felt much more secluded there. "It can't stand, and we don't have to worry about it standing above and searching with its tentacles anymore."

Lewis went quiet for a moment then raised his eyebrows. "We are not finished with the machine yet, Mrs Steed. We are not going to bring about its end by skulking in the woods. If you want to retreat there with your lads while we go on, then that's fair enough. But we want to finish this. We have to, Mrs Steed."

"But the thing is surely finished, Mr Puttnam. Why risk your life further by trying to do more?"

"We want it dead, Mrs Steed, and there has never been a better opportunity to kill one. I'm going back to hear what the quartermaster has to say. He and his crew have fought against the machines before. They have seen them destroyed."

Mrs Steed looked to her son and grandson. She could see that, like all young men, they wanted to be in on the kill. It was against her protective instinct, but deep down she could feel their male needs wanting to do something. She reasoned that if men were good at anything, they were good at destroying and making a mess of things. She was surrounded by men who seemed to be making a jolly good mess of the Martian machine. The job was part done and they would want to complete the task. Typical men with their finishing touches, whatever it takes to complete.

"Let's get over there, then," she said reluctantly, and looked to Reg and Jimmy. "You two stick with me and don't go off anywhere without me. Do you understand?"

They nodded in agreement and then followed Lewis. Swiftly, they all clambered over the wall and passed the fallen trees. They were quickly at the cottage wall where Llewellyn, Blanc and Bisset were gathered.

Blanc was shaking and prattling nervously to Bisset in French. He was gesticulating with his arms and pulling faces as he spoke, the way foreign people appeared to communicate.

"Mr Blanc, I presume," cut in Mrs Steed, feeling that foreign people had no reserve. The quaint looking French seaman was covered in dirt and plaster. His black beard and moustache were white from the dust. His uniform was torn and bloodied.

The old quartermaster stopped and looked at the dirt-encrusted English woman. Her hair was hanging in rats' tails with an unkempt updo on top, and there was dust all over her. There was congealed blood along the side of her forehead and her dress was filthy and torn in many places. Yet still she held herself with feminine grace.

"You must be Mrs Steed." Quartermaster Blanc bowed his head slightly, in polite acknowledgement. "I am very pleased to meet you. Even under such dire circumstances."

"That's putting it mildly," Lewis jested.

Mrs Steed observed the restraint and polite demeanour that was very much a part of Quartermaster Blanc. She was pleasantly surprised when he addressed her in English. "It is reassuring to know you too, Quartermaster Blanc."

"I am pleased to know you are safe, Mrs Steed. It was P.C. Llewellyn's desire that we come here. He was most concerned about you." He smiled, and his thick bushy moustache rose amid the dirt-encrusted wrinkles of his weathered face. "I'm also pleased that you and your family are well."

She smiled and looked to P.C. Llewellyn, grateful for the policeman's concern, before turning back to Blanc. "As well as can be expected, Mr Blanc. I thank you all for coming. You are most welcome. Though it may not appear so," she laughed, and looked about at the fire and destruction.

Blanc smiled and nodded, understanding the lady. She had the usual English sense of humour.

All turned at the approach of Linville and Segal. They had moved forward towards the churchyard before the stricken machine began to fire its heat ray again.

"We thought you were dead," said Jimmy, as the two seamen stopped before the group, clutching their rifles.

They had found cover and now came scurrying back. Segal had a big smile on his face for the quartermaster. He offered him a water bottle. Blanc took it and offered Mrs Steed the first sip. She accepted gratefully then returned it. Another water bottle was produced by Linville and all took a swig.

"Excuse me," said Blanc and gulped at the water. He returned the bottle to his subordinate. "Merci."

Mrs Steed ventured to ask a question. "Mr Puttnam says that you have almost destroyed the fighting machine for good, is this so, Mr Blanc?"

Blanc looked at the old poacher and raised his eye brows. "You do me much credit, Mr Puttnam, perhaps too much."

Llewellyn stepped forward and added his support. "You've done a great deal already, Mr Blanc. More than I thought could be done. It seems pointless not to see the thing through. You have achieved so much. Can we now give this fighting machine the coup de grace?"

The French seamen added their voices of approval upon hearing the words "coup de grace". After all, Llewellyn had used French words.

Blanc turned to look at all the smiling faces. It had been a chorus of approval from everyone. He felt a little embarrassed by such well-intentioned adulation. As well as much humbled by the good people about him.

He held up his arms, for everyone's attention. "I think that much of what has been achieved was due to good fortune. Now the machine is down, we need to think how we might bring about the complete destruction of the creature inside." He looked to Mrs Steed. "Do you understand my meaning?"

"I do, Mr Blanc. We have a wounded animal in that contraption. It can still work part of the machine. It can and will lash out at anyone who dares to approach it. Would it die if we left it alone? It must be badly injured." She wanted to present the idea of doing nothing and letting nature take its course. "Others could die in a pointless attempt to kill a monstrous brute that you may have already mortally wounded."

"It might heal itself," added Lewis. "Supposing it could make repairs to the machine. It could get to its feet again?"

"I think Lewis could be right. Can we afford to take such a chance?" Blanc said. "The cannon is still back on the other side the hedge. I do not think the artillery piece was destroyed. I left shells in the ditch next to the gun. We could fire more shots into the fighting machine. After all, it is unable to move. It would make a perfect target where it is laying in the church yard. It will mean we must, once again, pass by the church wall to get beyond the hedge and stile."

Reg coyly put his hand up like a school child wanting to say something. Blanc regarded the mentally challenged young man and smiled politely.

"We will need to keep people this side while the cannon is fired from the stile," said Reg in a slow manner.

"We can do this," replied Blanc, not knowing what the simple man was getting at.

Reg continued. "When the machine is on fire, the Martian will get out and make for these cottages or the church tower. It will want to find cover. We will be able to shoot it."

Lewis nodded approvingly. "He's right. Reg has already killed one in the church."

Jimmy added his voice. "There were two of the Martians in the machine, and Uncle Reg killed one when we went into the church tower. It was before you arrived. When we rescued Granny."

A look of surprised awe came over Blanc's face. He regarded the simple giant with new respect. "You are surely a formidable man, Monsieur."

"He is too," added Jimmy enthusiastically.

Blanc smiled at the youngster, and then turned back to Reg. "I think we shall do things as you say, Monsieur. I will take P.C. Llewellyn and Bisset. Everyone else will wait here. We will load the artillery gun again. I'm sure we will get another close-range shot. If the Martian emerges, you have two shot guns and two rifles to administer the coup de grace."

All the men smiled and nodded their approval. About them was total destruction of what had once been a serene little English country village. The destroyed buildings were burning, the trees were burning and the vanquished church was burning with only the belfry standing.

Mrs Steed sighed. She knew much of men's plans from past memory. Men often achieved in the end. Yet she realised that supposed events, beforehand, were nearly always mere speculation. If she had learnt anything in her life, she knew things never went the same way from theory to actual event.

"Don't forget that the machine is still capable of shooting that heat ray back at you. Your cannon shot will have to count. You must keep the gun covered after firing. Because if that is destroyed, you will have no way of further damaging the machine."

Blanc frowned. "You are correct, Madame. We will need to fire the gun and then quickly move it before the fighting machine realises where the shot came from. We will then need to find another place to shoot from. We will not be able to use the same spot twice. However, we have an advantage. The crippled monster will always be at a fixed point. Unable to move away. Yet we can and will."

Llewellyn pushed his helmet back in a carefree manner. He looked the most unruly policemen who ever walked his beat. That he was still doing his duty in the apocalyptic landscape was comical – but also uplifting, and wonderful to behold. "You will have

The Last Days of the Fighting Machine

cover from the tall hedgerow and the dyke. The rise of the mound will be valuable cover. We must use it to good advantage."

"I agree, P.C. Llewellyn." Mrs Steed clasped her hands with excitement. Men will be men, yet somehow they would stumble upon a workable and constructive plan. They always did in the end. She had to support such fine spirits. Let them pursue their new hope.

The new mood of optimism was infectious. Mr Blanc smiled as he watched the British doing those things they were noted for doing best. Creating new opportunities, improvising during times of crisis. He was becoming increasingly excited at being part of it.

"We should set off now, Policeman Llewellyn." Blanc looked to Mrs Steed. "The rest of you must stay here. Keep your guns to the ready."

Lewis made a suggestion. "We should prepare ourselves in the rubble of your end cottage, Mrs Steed. If the Martian tries to get away from the machine and the artillery gun, it is unlikely to go forward to the church tower. It will seek cover in the rubble of your place. We will have a firing squad ready for the thing. We can lay in wait. Watch as the hideous sod gets out of the fighting machine."

Blanc agreed. "You good people do that. Policeman Llewellyn, Bisset and I will go to the artillery piece now." He looked to the policeman and, beneath the dust and congealed blood, he smiled reassuringly.

"Ready when you are, boyo." Llewellyn pulled the tip of his helmet down. His adrenalin was pumping and like, the rest, he harboured a strong belief that they could defeat the machine and the creature within. "I would like to see us bang a big nail into that coffin. Over the past weeks I have indulged little inklings. The suspicion has grown. And now I have real belief that we can overcome these creatures."

"Then hammer that nail home, P. C. Llewellyn," said Mrs Steed with bile for the Martians. "I would feel fulfilled if I saw that thing completely destroyed."

"To the stile then, Policeman Llewellyn. There is not a moment to lose," advised Blanc, beaming with enthusiasm as he gripped Bisset's shoulder reassuringly. The three crouched down and made their way along the front of the wrecked and burning terrace cottages towards the church, where the stricken machine lay.

CHAPTER 9

ATTACKING THE FIGHTING MACHINE

Mrs Steed and her group of people made their way into the public house. She wanted to go out into the back yard. The matriarch had decided to approach her end-terraced home via the back gardens, where there was the advantageous rear yard walkway, offering better cover.

"Take some of the oil lamps," whispered Lewis to Reg and Jimmy.

Along with Linville and Segal, they took a few lamps, some from the tables and the rest from the walls.

Soon the small party had left the public house and followed Mrs Steed along the walkway. The sound of fire and destruction all around. When they had reached her cottage, she cautiously opened the gate and they all sneaked across the back yard to where the rear door had been. It was blown out and resting against the side wall of the yard. Inside, the kitchen no longer had an opposite wall – it was blown in. They stumbled across the rubble towards the shattered opening, guns held in readiness. Through the hole in the kitchen wall there was a clear view of the ruined churchyard and the belfry tower, as well as the wreckage of the giant Martian fighting machine. Its huge compartment was leaning against the tower's stone wall like a twisted head. Smoke was billowing out of various joints and shell ruptures. Brick, stone and small fires were in scattered abundance.

"Keep down," whispered Lewis.

Linville and Segal stopped, waiting for his guidance. Mrs Steed pointed to cover for Reg and Jimmy. Then she turned back to Lewis, knowing the old rogue's mind was beginning to click into motion.

"What now, Mr Puttnam?" she asked, and for once she seemed to want one of his fiendish little ideas, which in more amiable times had been the talk of the village.

He was about to answer when there was a bellow from the machine.

Alooough!

The hideous call boomed out through the smoke-filled air. Despite its thunderous quality, it was strangely devoid of menace, almost moaning – as though calling out for pity. Everyone had instinctively gone to the ground amid the loose bricks and smashed kitchen utensils. For a moment, they all feared their presence had been discovered. But their alarm diminished quickly. They were less frightened of the Martian now.

Lewis lifted his head cautiously and chanced a look through the gaping hole in the kitchen wall. The machine lay stricken and immobile in the cemetery grounds, amid gravestones and rubble. He caught sight of Blanc, Llewellyn and Bisset on the further side of the grounds, beyond the destroyed church. His excitement swelled as they clambered over the stile.

"The other group have reached the field piece," he whispered delightedly.

"Good," replied Mrs Steed excitedly.

"There has been no response call from other machines," said Lewis. "No other Martian will be coming to this thing's aid."

"That machine is alone, then," muttered Reg.

"That's right, Reggie," replied Lewis. "And that thing knows it."

"What were you thinking about before the Martian called out, Mr Puttnam? There was something on your mind. I could tell by the sly look on your face," Mrs Steed said. There was excitement in her tone.

Lewis smiled. "Well, Mrs Steed. Are we game for anything devilish I might think of?"

"Of course, Mr Puttnam. Especially if it can be used against that machine out there."

"I want the oil lamps." He held one up and pointed to the rest that each man carried. "I thought we might make a fire around the machine. If we can get a good enough fire going, we might be able to heat things up inside the machine. That Martian will either stay, to cook inside, or be forced to come out."

"If it comes out, it won't last long," added Reg, gripping his scythe in one hand and his double-barrelled shotgun in the other.

Mrs Steed went straight to a pantry and came out with two more oil lamps. She looked to the French sailors and gestured. There was a nod of approval. A plan for an attack of fire against the Martian was to everyone's liking.

CHAPTER 10

BACK TO THE FIELD GUN

Blanc and Llewellyn went along the churchyard wall with swiftness and comparative ease. They crawled right under the sprawled machine's line of sight. They had just made it to the stile when the call of the machine had boomed out across the tortured ground.

Llewellyn put his hands to his ears as the noise went through him. "That was loud," he cursed.

Blanc looked as though he was in discomfort from the pitch of the Martian cry. "It was almost pitiable. Like a distress call."

Bisset looked through the burnt and blackened foliage to the enormous collapsed mechanism. He pondered the creature trapped inside. Then he looked across the empty fields, where the sickly pink patches appeared to be yielding to the new offensive of green vegetation.

"There is nothing responding. No interest from other Martians," said Quartermaster Blanc.

"I don't think there is likely to be," replied P.C. Llewellyn. "Everything is retreating. Even the red weed. It stands out a mile. Everywhere we look, the Martian weed is turning pink, losing its vibrant red colour and dying. Our own greenery is coming back. Our hopes are too."

Blanc smiled and nodded his head. "Let us prepare the gun and put another shell into that monster."

"You're talking my language there, Mr Blanc." Llewellyn had a little dust upon him, but apart from that he still looked the picture of upright Victorian values in his uniform. He pulled the tip of his helmet forward once again, so that it rested neatly upon his head, then he adjusted the chin strap. He also wriggled his nose, as though adjusting his neatly trimmed moustache.

They moved towards the stile and clamoured over. Then cut along the pathway through the bank where the artillery piece stood. The fires from the heat ray were gone. Only blackened and smouldering hedgerows remained.

"The cannon is still here," Blanc said with a hint of glee. "The machine walked past this weapon twice. Once when it tried to use the river water to put out its flames. And again, when it came back to the village in pursuit of me. "

"Well, it's fortunate that it's undamaged," replied Llewellyn.

Blanc jumped down into the ditch before the dyke and lifted the heavy box containing the last few shells. "Only three left. We must make the most of them."

"I'll let you load, Mr Blanc. I haven't got a clue how this thing works. Police training never prepared us for artillery shooting." Llewellyn was keen, and his excitement was growing. The Martian was crippled and unable to pursue them. He now felt more confident about what was coming.

"Remember, it still has its heat ray, and we will need to retreat behind this bank in order to avoid it," Blanc reminded them.

The old quartermaster looked about the area to reassure himself. There would be enough cover. He opened the breech and removed the spent shell casing. He then slid a new shell home and locked the breech.

Together, they slowly wheeled the cannon towards the stile and began to check and lower the gun barrel. On the previous occasion, the fighting machine had been standing. Now it was lying on the ground. Nervously, each man glanced at the wreckage of the machine, making sure there was no movement from its heat ray apparatus. A big section of the body trunk protruded above the wrecked church wall, lying against the belfry tower. It was a big target at such a close range to aim at.

Carefully, Blanc began to check the sights. It would be easy to hit the exposed section of the machine's trunk, but the top bar of the stile forced the gun's barrel too high.

"We need to get the barrel beneath the first shaft of the stile. If we put the barrel above the top one, the shell will go over the machine. It will miss."

Resigned, the three men dropped the gun barrel a little. As they wheeled the cannon forward again, they realised the circumference of the gun was slightly too big to pass between the top and second beam of the stile. The shell would just about pass through, but not the actual barrel. It was a fraction too wide.

"We must press the metal lip of the gun barrel against the top and bottom planks. The shell will pass through." Blanc said.

"We are lucky that the ground rises beyond the wall," whispered Llewellyn. He watched the machine intently, aware of how exposed they were.

"We must push the gun back to the cover of the bank wall the moment we fire, Policeman Llewellyn." There was a concerned tone in Blanc's voice. "Firing the gun will be the easy part. The main task would be preserving the artillery piece. We must move it behind the bank to reload. It will involve commitment and risk."

"I hope we hit the blooming thing then," muttered Llewellyn. "That might buy us a few moments before it can respond."

Blanc checked the sightings again and then firmly took hold of the firing mechanism. He looked to Llewellyn. Dust and congealed blood were caking his weathered features. "Ready?"

"When you are, Mr Blanc."

Bisset put his hands to his ears and opened his mouth. Llewellyn decided to copy the young seaman.

Blanc pulled and the field gun boomed. The three men allowed the weapon to kick back before throwing themselves upon it. Quickly wheeling it back to the cover of the grassy bank. Behind them, the explosion had erupted. Flame and debris climbed up and out across the already strewn graveyard. They had not had time to survey the impact of the shot, but they were sure the shell had struck the target.

They had just reached the cover of the dyke wall when the shrill whirring sound that the heat ray apparatus made before discharging its deadly hot beam of energy could be heard.

"Quick, run further along the dyke! We can leave the gun for the moment."

Blanc pulled at the policeman's arm, and both made their way nimbly along the dyke wall as the heat ray ripped through the tall hedge and into the scarp of the mound behind which they had taken cover.

Fire and earth flew up into the air as a line of explosions tore up along the embankment, forcing

Blanc, Bisset and Llewellyn to dive to the ground. Turf and soil cascaded down from the opposite side of the knoll covering them as the trail of upsurge passed by and moved further along the bank.

Coughing and spluttering, Llewellyn clawed his way out of the soft earth and threw off his helmet. He turned to Blanc and began to frantically pull and dig away at the sliding earth that had toppled over the quartermaster. Bisset came to his aid. Eventually, they managed to get Blanc's arms and head free. They continued at speed until the trapped man was completely unrestricted. All were gasping for breath. Their eyes bulged with fear. It had been a narrow escape.

"I wonder if we are pushing our luck a bit, Mr Blanc." The policeman was looking very dishevelled and dirty now and his clean-cut British-bobby look was gone.

Blanc sneezed then began to laugh at the sight of the policeman. "Welcome to the club, Mr Llewellyn – come on in the water is lovely."

"Oh, I look more like you now do I, Boyo?" He smiled, and looked back at the gun. "We are going to have to do a little digging to get that old girl out."

Blanc turned and saw that soil had entrapped the wheels of the cannon, but it was not too bad. "We will be able to dig that out, but first let us see what damage we have done."

The Last Days of the Fighting Machine

Llewellyn smiled. "Let's do so indeed."

Like naughty and excited school boys the three of them scampered to the top of the dyke wall and cautiously peered over the summit. The line of hedgerow was gone – sliced away by the heat ray. However, it gave them a clear view of the stricken tripod. It lay burning upon the rubble of the church, surrounded by further carnage and destruction. Its undercarriage was in flames where the leg joints were connected. One of the linkage parts was broken, with severed cables hanging from it, and the broken long limb was amputated and lying useless at the bottom of the rubble, stretched out among the boulders and head stones.

"Well, it certainly can't walk anywhere now," whispered Llewellyn. "A very commendable shot, Mr Blanc."

He smiled modestly. "Thank you, Policeman Llewellyn." He looked along the embankment and began to think of the shot they could have from upon the bank. "The gun is not the biggest of pieces, and I'm wondering if we could get the thing up the rise."

Llewellyn suddenly became concerned. "We would be very exposed, Mr Blanc, and we would have to aim and fire very quickly."

"I know, but a little way along over there," he pointed along the slope. "The rise is not steep and we might get the gun up and be able to fire down into the machine. One good shot into the green window thing at the front. The shell might go through and explode inside the machine. The Martian inside will be killed surely, and the task will be complete."

"I've a feeling that I'm being charmed into this," replied Llewellyn, concerned yet resigned. "Come on then, let's get to it. I don't want to have too much time to dwell on this one."

All three were suddenly alert to the sound of breaking glass. They turned to see that oil lamps were being hurled at the stricken machine. As the lamps shattered, small fires erupted over the body trunk.

"It's Lewis and Mrs Steed's group," replied P.C. Llewellyn. "They are throwing oil lamps at the machine."

"If it fires its heat ray back at them...?" Blanc added without completing the sentence. "We must fire while its attention is diverted."

⇁⇁

There was a distinct note of panic in Mrs Steed's voice as she ushered Jimmy and Reg back out of the kitchen door into the yard. "Quick, Mr Puttnam, I think we have overstayed our time in here. That thing will be onto us at any moment."

"Three hits out of four, Mrs Steed," replied Lewis. "The thing is burning. That heat will get through the body trunk surely."

"Please come now, Mr Puttnam. Mr Blanc and P.C. Llewellyn have hit it again with the cannon. Perhaps we do not need to throw the oil lamps as well?"

"So that the Martian knows it has people attacking from both sides, Mrs Steed. I'm trying to divert its attention so that the gun crew can get a second loading for another shot."

"The machines seem very resilient. It is the creature inside you need to get at. You are just agitating it. Tell the two Frenchmen they must leave now, before they throw more lamps." Mrs Steed pointed to Segal, as he stood upon the rubble to cast another of the lamps through the gaping hole in the wall.

The sailor staggered slightly as he brought back his arm and hurled the burning lamp through the wall breach and out across the graveyard towards the stricken machine. The old lamp light hit the burning body trunk and shattered. More burning oil spread about another section of the fighting machine's trunk. A small cheer followed as Segal turned to leave. He had seen Lewis gesture emphatically to be away. It was the last thing he would see.

The hot ray of light tore through the wall rupture and hit Segal. The only scream came from Mrs Steed, as the intense heat forced everyone back towards the kitchen door. It was all so instantaneous

– but the vision was clear and precise. One moment the French sailor was there, and in the next instant his flesh and clothes were devoured in a swift radiance that left his blackened skeleton collapsing to the rubble – smouldering and hissing.

"Out! Out now!"

Lewis pushed Mrs Steed into the yard, where her son and grandson forced her towards the backyard door. The very one by which they had entered the place a few minutes earlier. Behind came Lewis and the remaining French sailor, Linville.

"That was not one of your better ideas, Mr Puttnam," scolded the old widow.

"We will not know yet, Mrs Steed. The thing is still burning. I don't think the creature inside can hold out. There is fire and destruction all about the machine. It must be doomed."

They made their way back along the rear yard communal walkway. At the end they stopped to gather their wits and catch their breath. There was no further sound of the heat ray apparatus accelerating up to discharge its deadly beam. However, they were excited by the sound of the artillery piece booming a second time.

"They've loaded the gun," said Reg. "I hope they got the blooming thing, Mum."

Lewis put his hand on Mrs Steed's arm. "Mr Linville and I must go back. We need to help

The Last Days of the Fighting Machine

Llewellyn and Mr Blanc. You wait here with your boys, Mrs Steed."

⟛

Once again, Llewellyn, Blanc and Bisset moved back down the bank. They were committed to the next stage of their attack upon the crippled metal monster. All about them was total devastation. Fire and smoke coming from what had once been the humble and beautiful little village of Paglesham Churchend. When they reached the gun, each man threw himself into digging and clawing away at the loose soil around the wheels. Quickly, they had freed the weapon. Blanc once more locked and loaded a shell into the breach and soon they were moving the field gun along the bottom of the embankment towards the gentler rise of the slope.

"This one is going to be a little tricky," said Llewellyn, still unconvinced by what they were trying to do.

"If we see the tripod's heat ray rise, we abandon the gun and take cover behind the bank." Blanc took a deep breath and licked his dry lips. "But its attention is upon the cottage where Lewis and Mrs Steed are. I think it has fired its heat ray there."

"Perhaps they have bought us time diverting the thing's attention," added Llewellyn.

Young Bisset was muttering prayers in French, whispering and crossing himself.

Slowly the three men heaved the cannon forward up the slope – feeling the strain of the weapon as it inched onto the top of the mound. Again, the exposure and vulnerability of their position was very apparent. They looked out across the churchyard. For a moment their resolve deserted them and they went to ground back behind the mound. The gun stood abandoned overlooking the devastation of the stricken machine and the scattered rubble of the church. The machine appeared unable to stand or move away from the spot it had collapsed onto.

"The Martian doesn't seem to be aware of us," whispered Llewellyn. He turned to Blanc. "What do you want to do?"

The old seafarer squinted, looking more intently beyond the fighting machine. Then he looked towards the backyards of the cottages.

"I can see the others," he said with surprise. "Lewis and Linville are creeping towards the perimeter of the church grounds from the back of the gardens. Look!" He pointed.

Llewellyn frowned. "What the devil are they up to now?" he hissed in concern. "Where are the others?"

"I don't know, but they are getting dangerously close to the machine and we know it still has its heat ray. They are exposed, and they'll be cooked if it targets them."

Blanc looked to the cannon nervously, then said. "You stay here. There is nothing you can do. I need to aim and fire, which I can do alone."

Llewellyn offered no argument and turned his scrutiny to the others. Lewis and Linville were creeping forward along the rear walkway to the backyards. He pursed his lips and silently vented his anger at them. "Get back, Lewis, or you'll be roasted, you blithering fool." He watched on, astounded. Lewis brought his arm back and slung something over the small privet bush at the end of the alley and into the church grounds. Then Linville did the same. Llewellyn's eyes widened in disbelief as the objects landed around and upon the burning body trunk, erupting with more flames. As the liquid ran across the alien trunk, so did the spreading flames. More fire danced wickedly upon the strange alloy shell of the incapacitated fighting machine capsule.

Lewis and Linville turned and scrambled back down the alleyway. During the confused retreat, Lewis fell.

The machine reacted swiftly. It raised one of its spines. The one gripping the apparatus that fired its heat ray. Llewellyn squinted and gasped. In a moment the device would begin to whirl up before the shaft of wicked and heated light discharged.

"Run, blast you, Lewis!" muttered the policeman.

Lewis had only just managed to get shakily to his feet. His face frozen in fear. He looked up at the rising mechanism. The hideous device that discharged the dreaded heat ray. He gulped while trying to walk backwards. A man that knew death was upon him. The shrill whir suddenly started. The funnel was charging up ready to fire. Lewis stopped, knowing that his moment had come.

Before the heat ray could discharge, Blanc pulled the firing mechanism of the field gun. The canon boomed again. The shell ripped into the concave green orb of the fighting machine's front viewer. It was hard to tell if the green hazy substance was organic membrane or something more solid and artificial. For a split second, a hole momentarily appeared. The green tissue ruptured and then the orb exploded outwards amid flame and mucus. The fighting machine's heat ray jolted upwards. It discharged a javelin of burning energy up into the smoke-filled sky, screeching through the air like a thunder bolt. Then the spine tentacle went limp and fell back upon the burning alloy with a loud clang.

The machine was being devoured by further, more intense, flames and Llewellyn muttered. "Nothing can be alive inside of that – surely not?"

Blanc had jumped down beside him for cover. "I agree with you, Mr Llewellyn. The shell has exploded inside the machine and whatever is inside could not escape the impact of the confined explosion."

"I know what you say makes sense, but somehow I don't feel too confident about it."

Then, as though to lend emphasis to the policeman's words, the Martian speaker system hollered out from the burning wreckage. High-pitched alien howling rang out over the debris into the smoke-filled sky.

Aloough!

"I do not believe this," cursed Blanc frustrated. "How much more can that thing take?" He peered over the slope into the flaming machine and watched in horror as its tentacles suddenly whipped out and began to attach to headstones.

Llewellyn looked too. "Good God, those things are being used to drag it away from the church ground."

The flaming alloy began to creak – protesting as the trunk pulled itself upright into what seemed a sitting position. Then, like a wounded beast, the enormous machine dragged its wrecked and burning carcass across the graveyard. The grating of alloy and grinding mechanics screamed out in protest, as the gargantuan monster moved towards the hedgerow.

Blanc, Llewellyn and Bisset watched in horror. It was an unbelievable sight. Thick, black smoke poured from the alien mechanism's ruptured front window while fires burned beneath and above. It was hard to fathom out how anything could be inside controlling the machine. The creature should be dead. Nothing could have survived. Yet still, the ungainly titan heaved and hauled its way towards the charred and burnt hedge where the old stile was.

"Let's get away from here."

Llewellyn descended the embankment with Blanc and Bisset following. They abandoned the gun at the top of the mound, and after retreating a little way they turned to watch. They heard the clamour of screeching metal smashing through what remained of the hedgerow barrier. One of the machine's tentacles came up over the top of the embankment and reached out to grab the artillery piece. The field gun was lifted angrily into the air and then slammed down with colossal force. As it smashed into the earth with the wheels breaking in various parts, the barrel bounced onto the red and green grass. On the other side of the mound, they knew the giant machine was hauling itself ever closer.

"It looks like we are all out of shots," muttered Llewellyn not daring to take his eyes from the waving tentacle that had come up from the hidden side of the mound.

"Let's slowly back away while we think of what to do next." Blanc put a hand upon the policeman's shoulder. "Come my friend, I think that machine will try to crawl past this point to the river." He looked to the inlet and noticed the tide was beginning to come in. "That is what it did last time."

On the other side of the embankment they could only hear the machine as it came closer. The colossal grinding sound grew louder. Then the wrecked and smoking machine suddenly appeared. The diabolical structure emerged over the top of the mound, a deranged and injured metallic beast churning earth as it dragged its huge mass onwards. The wreck of the field gun was buried by the vast landslide. Enormous appendages reached forward and hooked deeply into the soil. Then it crudely hauled its monstrous frame forward. The damaged limbs and body were groaning in protest with every laboured movement. The wrecked titan heaved itself up and over the embankment dragging two of its huge smashed legs behind.

Llewellyn, Blanc and Bisset doubled back over to the stile once the Martian mechanism had passed. They watched the huge crippled limbs dragged in the giant furrow of the machine's track.

"We must get back to the pub," said P.C. Llewellyn.

"Pub? Oh yes," replied Blanc. "The public house."

The three men jogged back to the village where they knew the rest of the group would be.

Lewis staggered back into the yard of the public house. His face was drained. How close he had come to death. They could hear the machine's alloy grinding in protest and fading as it pulled its way out of the churchyard.

"That thing is dragging itself away towards the creek," he stuttered nervously.

"Good God, Mr Puttnam, that was a reckless thing to do," said Mrs Steed offering him a glass of whisky. "I have seen fit to commandeer such tonic from the premises of the public house." The dusty and dishevelled lady had a tray with more glasses and was offering another to Linville. Reg took one and so Jimmy chanced his luck.

"Only the one young man," his grandmother scolded. Usually she would not entertain the idea of alcohol, but she reckoned the circumstances merited it. "I do hope that P.C. Llewellyn, Mr Blanc and Mr Bisset are all right."

As though on cue, the three men came into the yard via the side alley from the front. All looked traumatised. Llewellyn spoke first. "We put two more shells into the thing and still it keeps moving." He then thankfully accepted a whisky from Mrs Steed's tray. "One of its legs is missing but it is using its tentacles to pull itself along. It is making for the creek where it will be able to put out the flames and stop the smoke."

"I saw its heat ray arm drop after you hit it," said Lewis. "Does that mean it can't use the weapon anymore?"

"We can't tell for sure," replied Llewellyn. "But I would not count on it yet."

Mrs Steed offered Blanc and Bisset the tray of whiskies. "Waste not, want not," she said. Blanc and Bisset took a glass each. "What happens now?" she asked.

Lewis spoke. "We still have oil lamps and alcohol."

Blanc answered quickly. "We can't get too close. The tentacles will take us. Even if we cause it to burn, the thing will be able to put the flames out with water."

Llewellyn agreed. "It is by the inlet now, Lewis. Fire is no longer a viable option."

"We need something else," said Lewis. "We have come this far and the machine is all but finished. If we could get close enough to throw something through that smashed front window part of the machine. Something that can explode."

P.C. Llewellyn sighed. "We have put a shell through the window already. But perhaps something else might finish the job. The thing must be badly injured inside the cabin."

Lewis drank another whisky and put the empty glass on Mrs Steed's tray. "We need a fuse, a bottle and the powder from the shotgun cartridges." He turned to Reg. "There must be a good few in that bag. Did you get them from under the Walker's staircase?"

"We needed to get them to rescue Mum," replied Reg guiltily. "We weren't trying to steal."

Lewis smiled and held up a placating hand. "That's all right, Reg. You and young Jimmy were more than welcome, and I am pleased you did so. Right now, I want to take a few cartridges and get the powder from them. I've got an idea."

"Is it one of your more devious ones, Mr Puttnam?" Mrs Steed was once more supportive of Lewis and his mischievous abilities.

Lewis grinned. "It is so cunning you could iron the lad's shirts with it, Mrs Steed. I will also need some nails to mix in with the powder."

"Why?" Reg was bemused by the old poacher's antics.

Lewis looked up at everyone. "With nails and gunpowder inside a glass bottle and an explosion in a confined space! Well, it's going to do a great deal of damage to anything that is in the way. Even a blooming Martian."

"I hope so," replied Blanc. "But we have already had one shell explode inside the machine. Yet still, it moves."

"I can only put that down to bad luck," Lewis answered. "Maybe the creature inside is badly injured, like the damaged machine. One more try and we could finish it for good. Even if it doesn't work, I doubt it would make the Martian's situation better. The way I see it, we have nothing to lose by trying."

"I hope that the heat ray is out of action," added Blanc.

"We still need to be careful of the tentacles," reminded Jimmy.

"Yes," agreed Mrs Steed. "We saw what it did to one of your crewmen, Mr Blanc. It was dreadful." She shook at the ghastly memory of the wretched sailor. How he was held in the air as his blood was sucked from him.

"That is the one concern," agreed Lewis. He began to tip the gunpowder out of the shells. "I will have to sneak up on the thing."

Llewellyn had an idea. "We could cause some form of diversion from the mound overlooking of the inlet."

"How?" asked Blanc.

Llewellyn took off his police helmet and mopped his brow with his handkerchief. "Even if we start shooting at the thing, it will try to attack with its tentacles. It will try to reach out at us while Lewis sneaks up from another direction. We must make sure we stand well back. Well out of reach of those things."

Mrs Steed looked concerned. "P.C. Llewellyn, we don't know how far the machine's arms can reach. Except that it is a long way. I have witnessed this. They are taller than fully grown trees, and can scoop people from the ground. That we do know."

"We need to take some form of risk." Llewellyn looked for acknowledgement from the others. Blanc's men stared at him confused. They could not understand a word of what was being said. "Can you explain what we are thinking of doing, to your men, Mr Blanc?"

Immediately, the old quartermaster began to explain the plan in French to Linville and Bisset. They replied with questions of their own, and one volunteered to make a stable fuse for Lewis' bomb. Something the old poacher was most grateful for.

Once everything was prepared, Llewellyn went with Blanc and his crewmates back to the stile. Lewis remained with Mrs Steed, Reg and Jimmy. He was looking at his three homemade bombs in bottles.

"Three little bottle-based bombs of Greek fire."

Lewis was looking very pleased with himself.

"What is Greek fire?" asked Jimmy.

Lewis grinned. "Something that breaks and spreads fire, I think. Probably something the Greeks used, but I doubt this is the mixture. I also doubt they had bottles."

"Maybe pots or jugs," Reg suggested.

"Could be right, Reg." Lewis smiled at the simple man.

Mrs Steed was trying to be humorous. "Well, we've not had visitors for a very long time now. Where did you bump into that little lot? All those French seamen?"

Lewis chuckled and told her about his surprise at seeing P.C. Llewellyn cycling along the lane as though it was a normal day on the beat. Mrs Steed laughed at the absurdity of it all. She told Lewis of the few times Llewellyn had cycled into the village of late. A well-dressed country policeman, going about his duties as though everything was normal, in a red and green landscape. Their laughter ran its course. Then for a moment they both stopped. Reg and Jimmy looked on.

"Thank God he did his rounds and carried on, though." Mrs Steed was reflective and her mood changed. A tear came to her eye.

"Yes, it was very fortunate indeed," agreed Lewis. "If anyone ever says to me, 'you can't find a copper when you need one', I'll punch him right on the blooming nose."

"I'll help you," said Reg with a childish smile.

Again, they all laughed and made ready to walk along the backyard walkway.

"Be careful now, Mr Puttnam," said Mrs Steed warmly.

"I will – I promise."

She turned to Reg and Jimmy. "We will accompany Mr Puttnam to the church."

Together they went along the back walkway towards the church grounds. No one spoke anymore. There were no appropriate things to say. Lewis had a very dangerous task before him, one that he might not survive. As they pushed through the rickety old privet hedge, the smouldering debris of the old church was all about the graveyard. Massive undulations led towards the opposite perimeter, through the smashed hedgerow, where the fighting machine had dragged itself away and over the embankment. One of the machine's huge alloy legs lay across the church rubble, stretched out across the graveyard. Severed conduits ran along the limb joints and disappeared into the intersection. They looked like veins that fed the mechanical junctions. The sight was strange and unsettling. They were all used to the tall hedgerow hiding anything on the other side and now they could see the old mound wall. Beyond, in the distance, was the ominous sight of the broken fighting machine.

They stepped carefully over shattered headstones as they made their way across the desolation. Lewis and Mrs Steed stepped into the huge furrow that the machine had left and began to walk along it while about them, small fires flickered. Smoke from various places rose into the grey, polluted sky.

Jimmy stopped close to the bell tower. Amid the fallen brick and boulders at the base of the structure. He made out the exposed arched entrance. The door had been left open when they fled the church. Now it was broken from its hinges and lying over the debris. He looked up the staircase of the smashed building's standing tower. He reflected on how, only hours ago, he and his uncle had ventured into the steeple in search of his grandmother.

He peered into the dark opening and shuddered, feeling a tingling run up his spine. It was almost as though he thought something was staring at him from the black confines of the arched entrance. It was a fearful and yet compelling feeling, as though everything inside his head screamed at him to move on. Yet somehow, he felt drawn. His ears and eyes strained, trying to identify any sight or sound that might emit from the murky outlet. For a moment he thought he heard something. Whimpering! Distant far-off whimpering, like that of a lost animal alone and fearing the intruding blackness. He sensed it came from down the staircase as opposed from the ascending one they had used.

He jumped as Reg's hand gripped his shoulder. "Jimmy, come on. We need to keep up with my mum."

The youngster gulped as he came back from his bleak imaginings. "Sorry, Uncle Reg, I was lost in thought." He walked, on following in the footsteps of his grandmother and Lewis.

As they got to the top of the mound, the sight before them was awesome. The furrowed trail led out to the inlet, where the wrecked tripod was lying upon its side, immersed in the black silt and rising water of the incoming tide. Thick black smoke poured from several parts of its body trunk. Above it, three tentacles sprayed water that was somehow being sucked from the river.

"It's drenching the flames," said Lewis. He pursed his lips and looked down at his crude bombs. Three old beer bottles.

Further out upon the flats of Wallasea Island they could see the French sailors and P.C. Llewellyn detouring in a wide arc to place themselves before the machine on the opposite bank.

"Any moment now, and I will be going to it," Lewis was trying to work himself up.

"You can do it, Lewis," urged Mrs Steed.

Lewis smiled at her. "That's the first time you've ever called me by my name."

She frowned, then whispered. "Make sure it's not the last, please."

He lent forward and kissed her upon the forehead, and laughed to himself. She was a sorry sight after the trials and tribulations of her day, but she was a strong lady of great dignity. Everyone in the village had known and respected her. He could not think of anyone better to be with at a moment when courage was needed.

The first volley of shots was heard. They directed their scrutiny to the other bank, where the decoy group were firing at the machine. It seemed oblivious to their attention. The machine just continued to spray itself. It was preoccupied with dousing the flames.

Lewis held up one of his homemade bombs, for Llewellyn and his company to see. He descended the bank towards the fallen machine. Some sort of suction device was bringing water up through some of the machine's appendages.

The French sailors with Llewellyn began to concentrate their rifle fire into the air. This was to avoid the risk of accidently hitting the old poacher.

Lewis nimbly made his way down the grassy mound. Stealthily, he made towards the smashed and burning Martian body trunk. One hand was raised, clutching a bottle bomb. The other was holding his shotgun. The poacher surveyed the colossal length of the useless prostrate limbs that were sinking in the silt, only emerging towards the undercarriage of the fighting machine's body trunk. He marvelled at how long the strange limbs were. Then at how distant his goal still was. He willed himself on, holding his bottle bomb ready. The sight of three tentacles arced above the smoking body trunk. Hissing with the spray of muddy water. It made him shudder. He feared that at any moment one would lash down at him, entwine him and lift him over the mud, to hold him while he was punctured and sucked dry of blood. He pressed himself to the huge horizontal leg and dismissed the thought. He began to follow the limb's course. The skills acquired from night-time poaching still worked in day light. What a strange sensation. His heart began to beat faster as he warily moved towards the undercarriage. He was searching for a convenient rupture in the body armour where he could put his bottle bomb. The sight of one of the flaying tentacles caused him to freeze. What if the mechanism had sight? The protuberance had to have some sort of ability. Such a device latched onto the French sailor when they were all hiding in the wood. It was not sight, but perhaps sound or movement that could be detected. Once again, Lewis dismissed the phobia and continued moving towards the wrecked alien abomination.

He gritted his teeth and willed himself on amid the sound of continued gun shots and water spray.

"Bless them," Lewis whispered to himself. The French sailors' efforts to divert the Martian's attention were appreciated.

The Last Days of the Fighting Machine

Why was the machine paying no heed to the armed men on the other bank? Why was it insensible to the intended torment? As he reached the trunk his body was soaked by the spray. A sudden downpour of cold muddy water. It cascaded down the scorched curves of the machine's alien alloy. He put a hand out and lightly touched the unpleasant, off-white metallic shell. It was smooth, even where the blackened scorch marks were. He quivered at its unearthly feel. Slowly, he looked up at the machine's curvature. The dirty water plummeting from the curves. He closed his eyes and felt the silt running down the wrinkles of his features. Behind his ears and along his jaw. Slowly he turned his gaze to the tentacles that were above him. Lewis realised they were oblivious to his presence.

Why?

It was as though the outlandish feelers were working with a neat regularity, an unnatural consistency. Lewis frowned. They were unable to do anything other than spray the muddy water. He edged his way along the machine, pressing his back to its revolting smoothness. It felt as though he was leaning up against the smooth shell of a gigantic beetle. He felt nauseous with disgust.

Never taking his look from the tentacles above, he inched his way on towards the gaping hole where the shattered green orb had bulged out. When he had observed tripods from a distance, he fancied the orb to be a green membrane. A porthole viewer of some sort. Upon the wrecked opening's circular ridge, green discharge seeped. A revolting residue that looked like a huge swab of mucus. Lewis could see where the containing green film had punctured and then blown out. It was when Blanc had fired a shell into it. He halted, knowing that the Martian was probably inside the machine. He did not want to alert it in any way to his presence. His heart began to pound at the thought, as he edged a little closer to the opening. His gaze flitted anxiously from the window hole to the tentacles above.

Lewis ignited the fuse on his bottle bomb, which fizzed wickedly. He turned bringing his hand round in an arc, releasing the bottle into the window. At that moment, he pressed his front against the alien structure. There was no time to reflect. The bomb exploded inside the machine. A violent shudder. Enough to knock him backwards into the silt. Fire and thick smoke poured from within.

Fear was etched on his face as he looked up at the tentacles. The shock to see they were still above and spraying the dirty water.

Slowly, Lewis stood. He was smothered in the thick black silt of the river inlet. The tide was coming in. But to this, Lewis was oblivious. It was the tentacles that captivated him. His jaw dropped. The intensity of his scrutiny was etched upon his features. He was baffled.

The Last Days of the Fighting Machine

"They are just running," he muttered to himself. "No one is working them. They are just running like clockwork. They are working by themselves."

His attention was taken by splashing from the opposite bank and he turned to see P.C. Llewellyn jumping into the inlet and wading unsteadily across.

"Are you all right, Lewis?" he called.

"Yes," he replied. "I'm fine, but there is something strange." He cautiously walked towards the smoking hole where he had thrown the bomb. The rest of the group began to jump into the inlet and wade across behind Llewellyn.

"Don't go too close," shouted Llewellyn. He was pointing up at the suspended appendages. Still spraying the muddy water.

The machine looked like a gigantic dead beetle.

"Apart from the water spraying out, I think it is already dead," said Lewis. "It is just running like a wind-up toy."

"We will need to take a look inside to make sure the Martian is dead," called Blanc as he approached the wrecked fighting machine.

"Be my guest." Lewis held out an arm as the French sailors cautiously approached. They moved forward crouching and pointing their rifles up distrustfully.

"Have you looked inside?" asked Blanc.

"No," replied Lewis nodding towards the smoke coming out of the machine. "I thought it would be best to let it die down a little." He looked back to the mound, where Mrs Steed was waiting with Reg and Jimmy.

Bisset and Linville ventured towards the smoking hole with their rifles at the ready. Llewellyn went forward with them. "Steady lads, don't take it for granted that the thing is dead," He said.

Blanc repeated the policeman's words in French and decided to join them. All were curious to see what an actual Martian looked like.

Lewis remained where he was. He watched as the others were engulfed by the thinning smoke. For some reason he was not keen to see what the actual alien looked like. He was anxious to be away from the wrecked machine. He waited for a few minutes, listening to the bemused tons of French emitting from the smoke. After a while, Llewellyn and Blanc came back to him. The Frenchman looking puzzled and concerned while the policeman wore a look of disgust.

"The inside of that machine is vile," said Llewellyn.

Blanc added. "It is also empty."

Lewis frowned but deep down he was not surprised. He looked up at the arched tentacles again as they continued to spray water down upon the smoking hulk. "I said that everything seemed to be working by some sort of clockwork."

"How could you tell?" asked Llewellyn.

"It is the way the feelers move. They move different when they were being controlled by a Martian. I know it sounds strange, but you get a feeling for such things."

"When do you think the thing got out?" Llewellyn turned to Blanc.

"I am thinking it may have been before we put the shell through the green window of the machine. We thought that would have killed it. Yet still the thing crawled to the river."

"How could it do that?" Lewis was mesmerised. "I can understand the thing's water pumps being left on so that it sprays. But crawling to water by itself is impossible. The machine can't think. It's not alive. I suppose Martian clockwork is better than ours. Their machines can travel from one planet to another. They can engineer better than we can."

Blanc looked back at him. "Neither is a train, Mr Puttnam, but if you get it going and jump off, it will continue to run along the tracks until its fuel is spent. If we abandon a ship and leave its engines running, it will also continue until its fuel is spent or it crashes into something."

"So, the Martian is still at large." Llewellyn looked back to the rise, observing that Mrs Steed and her lads were approaching cautiously. He called out to them as they came closer. "The Martian is not in the machine. We think this thing moved to the river by itself. Like a locked engine."

She came among them and nodded her head. Concerned, Mrs Steed accepted the fact. "What is it like inside?" she asked nodding towards the smoking machine.

"The inner walls are wet with gunge, as though they want to keep the inside wet, and the levers look like large bones from some huge animal. I'm not saying they are. It is just indescribable, really." Llewellyn sighed as though he was not satisfied with his description.

Blanc tried to lend help. "The controls and the inner wall looked as though it was grown rather then made. The wall lining had pipes that looked like veins from something living, while the entire wall had a film of wet residue. The levers looked as though they were made of a substance like teeth or bone."

"Calcium?" Mrs Steed suggested.

"Yes, like something made of calcium," added Llewellyn.

Jimmy walked forward, excited as things suddenly seemed to make sense to him. "The Martian is back at the church. It escaped into the arch doorway that leads down to the crypt via the tower. We went upstairs when we rescued Granny. We never went down. The machine was close to the door. It must have gone down. I'm sure it was watching us when we passed by." He turned to his Uncle Reg. "It was the place I was looking at when you told me to keep moving." He then turned to his grandmother. "It is in there, Gran, honestly it is. I could swear that I heard a whimpering coming from the opening. I tried to peer in, but it was too dark."

Blanc shuffled, then looked back to the rising smoke from the church yard fires beyond the embankment. "It makes sense."

Llewellyn agreed. "The Martian got out when the shell hit home. It would have crawled for the nearest hiding place. The machine was already on the move. The Martian just left the contraption running. We were watching the fighting machine rather than the Martian that had abandoned it."

Blanc turned to his men who were still rummaging with the wrecked hulk of the tripod. The smoke and flame were all but extinguished. He called out instructions in French, telling them of the next task. He turned to Mrs Steed and said: "Before the day is out, Madame, we will kill the other Martian. The last one from this machine."

Behind the old quartermaster came the sound of rifle bolts locking as his men readied themselves to hunt the escaped alien.

Reg pulled out his scythe and nodded in the direction of the smoking tripod. "The creatures inside them machines are not so strong when outside." He had a grim but enthusiastic look, and no one was going to deny the simple man his opportunity to take part in the hunt.

His mother looked as though she was about to reprimand him. She wanted to make him stay. But Lewis put his hand gently upon her arm to restrain her from speaking out. She turned to meet the old poacher's gaze. Lewis lightly shook his head. After a moment of hesitation, she complied and remained silent.

CHAPTER 11

ONCE MORE UNTO THE BREACH

Again, the ragtag group cautiously approached the devastated church. Behind them was the derelict tripod, smouldering away beneath the water shower from its appendages that still worked. Smoke and fires were burning ahead of them in the graveyard. They walked on, amid the debris from the previous fighting. They no longer feared with the intensity of the past. When the tripod was properly functioning. Now, they were the hunters, and the Martian was the prey.

Llewellyn noticed the more daring aspect of each member of the group. He felt compelled to bring them down to earth a little.

"Don't get too confident now. We still do not know what we are up against. If the thing is cornered, it will be desperate and likely to lash out."

Blanc turned to Mrs Steed. "What do they look like, Madame?"

"I've only had fleeting glimpses of them. I was too terrified to scrutinise properly." She frowned, trying to build what description she could. "The closest we got was in the church tower. A few hours ago, before you people arrived. Reggie fought with one. It was behind the pews in the church. All we saw was a brief glimpse. My son killed the Martian thing. But the other was on the staircase. Hiding in the darkness. We did not stay in the church for long. We heard, rather than saw, the second Martian. It fled up the belfry and crossed the bridge onto the machine from the high tower window. When that happened, we were too preoccupied with getting away from the church. We fled as fast as we could. Before the church was destroyed by the heat ray. It caused most of this."

Blanc looked to Reg, who tried to elaborate. "All I saw was grey skin and its back. It was like a strange animal. It had long thin limbs, but I don't think it was very strong. I kept shooting into it."

"He shot it to pieces." Jimmy said. "But it was covered by the church pews and things happened very quickly. We did not get to look at it. It was probably unrecognisable after Uncle Reg had finished with it."

Blanc nodded, accepting what little they could tell him. "Well we need to enter the tower doorway,

The Last Days of the Fighting Machine

but if it has gone up the stairs; it cannot go too high. Eventually, the Martian will run out of church tower."

"The stairs also go down to a small crypt," Lewis said. "It might have gone below ground."

"Will you enter with some of my men and me?" asked Blanc.

"Yes," replied Lewis. He turned and looked to Reg. The simple man was abnormally big, and his physical presence would be assuring.

"I'll come too," added Reg. He looked to his mother. "I must be allowed to do this, Mum."

Her face was etched with concern, but in all his life he had never been more needed. And by people outside of his family. Suddenly, he was important. Her treasured son, who had been regarded with pity and sometimes cruelly mocked. Now he was needed. She would not take that away from him. He had already dispatched one of the Martians. He had some knowledge of what to expect.

"He has always been priceless to me," she felt compelled to say while looking at Lewis and Blanc intently. But for once she felt weak and at a loss. All her life she had been protective of her only son. She had already outlived her one daughter, who had left her a grandson. The thought of losing Reg terrified her.

Llewellyn came forward. "He is a big lad, Mrs Steed, and is by far the strongest of all here. There will be others with him, and all will be armed."

"I'm not going to stop him P.C. Llewellyn. I'm very proud of him but I am naturally concerned." She turned to her son. "You go ahead, Reg, and do us all proud."

Jimmy said. "There are candles in a hollow by the stairway. The vicar always kept candles there."

Reg smiled and unlocked his shotgun to check the cartridges in the barrel. He nodded his head to Blanc and followed the French quartermaster and Lewis. Llewellyn, Bisset and Linville remained with Mrs Steed and her grandson.

The search group found the candles and two small holders in the wall hollow, as Jimmy advised. They lit them and proceeded downstairs into the darkness of the tower stairwell. Then cautiously the three entered a dismal wrecked archway, slipping along the scattered boulders before they moved forward. Each spared a glance up the stairwell, before turning their attention to the claustrophobic hallway of darkness before them.

"Well," said Lewis. "Let's get on with it, then."

Each man felt his heart pounding. The danger of the unknown began to weigh heavily upon their thoughts. In the confines of the passage there was a growing intensity. The dim light from the burning candles spread along the walls, but there was also a thick dust. The glow could only penetrate for a few feet. They came upon a partial collapse of brick and stone. Momentarily, it blocked the group's progress. Then they noticed a narrow opening, and some blood.

"The creature has been here recently. These stones fell when the Martian machine destroyed the church," said Reg.

"No Martian could find refuge up the tower," added Lewis.

"I agree," replied Blanc.

Reg looked through the small gap. "The Martian could only go down the stairs." He looked to Lewis and Blanc. "If it wanted to hide…"

"Let us try to get through then. I will go first," added Blanc. He led the way, holding his candle stick up. He crouched down and went through the gap. Reg and Lewis followed. They continued along the narrow, winding course. The flickering flames of their candles caused their shadows to shudder on the stone walls. Gritting their teeth and willing themselves on, they moved cautiously into the ominous blackness. They all stopped when Lewis held up a hand, and remained silent. In the gloom, they had some sixth sense. Each man felt it. Lewis the poacher frowned as he strained to listen. Then they heard the faint whimper. As though distant in a far-off room. A rhythmic patter of tiny feet. The sound was edging closer. Almost as though there was an ill-deserved confidence in the approach. Lewis and

Blanc lifted their guns. They were ready to fire as the patter quickened and got nearer.

"It sounds like a dog," whispered Reg.

"A dog?" Blanc was confused.

Lewis hushed them impatiently as he strained to hear. Again, all fell silent for him. Finally, a look of hope spread across his features and he turned to face the rest. His eyes wide with astonishment.

"It sounds like Gippy."

Reg became a little excited and whispered. "It is. It's his little dog from the woods."

"All right," cut in Blanc taking control of the situation. "Let's be calm and not get too over-excited. We must remain alert and cautious."

The flame of Reg's candle flickered slightly. He put it down on the stone floor. Blanc and Lewis still held their lights as they tried to peer into the darkness. Reg clutched his scythe while gripping the shotgun with his other hand. He crouched, alert and ready. A menacing posture from which he could spring into action at any moment.

Lewis lifted his gun and pointed it in readiness for anything that might come out of the blackness. Blanc moved ahead of them, grimly determined to face anything that might occur.

Reg whispered a warning. "Watch the ceilings. It can crawl along above us. I've seen that before."

Blanc turned to him and frowned. "The ceiling?" he looked up fearfully, and cursed in French.

Cautiously, they resumed their advance. Their hearts pounding and the sweat of fear running down their backs. Again, they abruptly halted. Again, the sound of scampering feet approaching. Lewis and Reg pulled back the hammers on their shot guns but held the barrels to the floor. A safety precaution that both men followed when poaching. It was hard to maintain discipline under the strain of such confining anxiety. Blanc held up a restraining hand.

There was sudden joy as Gippy ran into the light. The French quartermaster breathed a sigh of relief. The old poacher knelt down and the little terrier jumped into his arms and began licking him and whimpering for attention, her tail wagging excitedly.

"Hush there, Gippy," whispered Lewis, trying to console the dog. "It's all right now, girl."

"Mr Puttnam, see if the dog will lead us to the Martian. The creature must have had hold of the dog and it may have let it go to distract us." Blanc looked up to the ceiling again.

"All right," replied Lewis, and he calmed the dog, cuddling and stroking it. "Gippy, show us where it is," he whispered with an encouraging tone. The little dog looked up at him, her ears upright, suddenly alert to her master's wishes. "Show us where it is, Gippy."

The little dog woofed lightly, aware that she could not bark loudly. Then she jumped out of

Lewis' arms with her tail slowly swishing to and fro. She looked up at them and slowly moved ahead towards the end of the light's feeble glow.

"Come on," said Blanc excitedly. "We must follow."

Each man's vision combed every part of the passageway that the candle light bathed. They moved forward, assuring themselves that nothing could pass them. They came into a large square room that was full of old church pews. Some sort of storage room. The old benches were untidily piled up against the far wall. It was also as far as anyone or anything could go. The last area bathed in their dismal candle light.

"It has to be in here," muttered Reg.

The fear become a growing manifestation of outrageous intensity. Pulsating in each man's chest and along their quivering arms. Let the Martian thing show itself. Let everyone get on with what must be done. For better or worse. End this waiting.

"I know the bloody thing is hiding somewhere in this room," Lewis hissed.

Blanc gave instructions. "Lewis, guard the doorway. Reg, please accompany me."

Lewis complied. So did Reg, moving tentatively forward with Blanc. They looked up at the ceilings and scanned about the walls bathed in the weak radiance of candle light. Then Blanc and Reg stopped before the benches. Alert and sure the Martian creature might be hiding behind the disused pews.

"Careful," Blanc whispered. "It must be hiding among the benches."

"Just like the last one," whispered Reg as he gripped his scythe and shotgun.

They heard Lewis behind them. He had nervously pulled back the lock on his gun and was whispering to Gippy to stay. The Frenchmen raised his army rifle. Each man began to sweat with profuse fear. The maddening anticipation was almost intolerable. The dreaded expectation that each yearned for. Anything to end the confounded dread. Anything to preoccupy the frightened mind. They wanted the foul thing to come smashing out at them. It felt as if the imposing darkness was squashing the dim light about them. The silence screamed out in each man's dismay and lingering trepidation.

Reg moved boldly forward clutching his shotgun in one huge hand with his thumb by the safety piece, his thick index finger against the triggers. He was ready to squeeze at the slightest provocation. The other hand pinned the handle of his scythe against the shotgun's barrel with its massive grip. His jaw locked and his face set grim. He peered at the piled and dusty pews.

"Careful, Reg," hissed Lewis from behind. "That bloody thing has got to be behind there."

Reg half turned to answer. But the words never left his mouth. The wooden benches exploded outwards and across the room. Shotgun flashes and a discord of excited shouts. Then the room was plunged into darkness. Another gun flash as Blanc's rifle went off almost bursting each man's ear drums. He had dropped his candle stick. Suddenly, every one began shouting in terror and excitement. A high-pitched unearthly screech tore out above the clamour. Blanc desperately tried to find his candle in the darkness. Lewis' candle had fallen back into the hallway as he staggered back. It had remained alight and he went to retrieve it. The pathway they had already come along was illuminated. But the store room was in darkness with the screams of the alien all about them.

Amid the confusion and terror, Reg had lifted his shotgun to shield himself. The end of a pew had swung out towards him. It had been an instinctive reaction to a fleeting glimpse. The furniture had hit the barrel as his gun went off, into the ceiling. He had fallen back winded, the pew crashing down onto him in the pitch black. But his strong, solid frame was able to dismiss the pain. Through his animal rage and fear, he roared. He had always fought fear with unadulterated anger. Blind fury. His mental defence system exploded inside his panic-stricken head. It instantly stimulated him. His desire to live, plus a strong hatred, energised an uncontrollable desire to kill.

With speed and agility, Reg instantly shot to his feet. With deep booming fury, howling like a huge angry bear, he raised his scythe blindly at the blackness. He comprehended the approach of something foul. He knew it was emerging from where the pews had been stacked. Reg sensed rather than saw the multiple appendages. The continuous unearthly shriek still afflicting his besieged ears.

Reg roared back, a deep bellowing rage. The brute force off the giant man's powerful swing smashed his scythe into something. It was a forward moving body of quivering repulsive flesh. The ghastly alien shriek raised to a new and more hideous crescendo. The Martian was stricken, and Reg felt the gratifying blood rush. His killer instinct ignited further. He took outrageous pleasure as his sharp scythe was impaled deep into the soft flesh of the unseen screaming Martian. He twisted and yanked at the blade's handle with gritted teeth.

The alien's agonised high-pitched torment intensified as it tried to recoil back. The sound of scattered pews mingled with the cacophony of the wailing Martian and human shouts. Reg went forward into the dark melee. He desperately clutched his embedded scythe. The blade was still skewered in the unseen creature. A hideous limb whipped out and thumped Reg in the side of the head. It was pathetic, and Reg knew it. The blow lacked power. Lingering squeals, like those of a brutalised and tortured hog, continued. The cries went up and down in volume as the giant man ripped his bloodied scythe free. In the blackness, Reg wickedly relished the sound of the ripping alien flesh. Again, the thin alien limb tried to fend him off. It gripped the side of his chin and Reg felt three long fingers spread out across his face. Long slimy fingers were trying to press into the crevices of his face, pressing and searching in vain for some kind of weakness.

Lewis was calling from behind, but he might as well have been a thousand miles away. "I'm getting the light, Reg. Don't worry mate. I'm getting the light."

Reg opened his mouth and sadistically bit into one of the probing slimy finger-like feelers, snarling like an angry lion as he did so. He shook his head and clenched his teeth tighter like a rabid dog, adding to the torment of the vile creature. The ugly bawling continued within the darkness, as did the panic-stricken cries of Blanc and Lewis.

"The thing is afraid," Reg yelled excitedly from his void. The alien's fingers ripped free. But Reg delighted in the knowledge. Again, he raised the scythe. Then delivered another thunderous blow into the soft sickly tissue of his unseen alien foe. The shrieking stopped, and all in the darkness heard the Martian start to choke and splutter. There was a desperate wheezing, as though gagging on the congestion caused by its own blood. Somewhere in the black, the hideous thing was clinging desperately to life.

Then came a fleeting moment of light, a flickering illumination. Lewis had grabbed his candle from the hallway and brought it into the room. The whole ghastly episode was before Reg. There, bathed in the glow, a huge body of gnarled grey looking blubber. It resembled a giant rotting potato. Large deranged eyes. Two yellow irises surrounding oval black pupils. They seemed to float on sickly off-white sclera. Above the deranged eyes were upturned black concave lenses on a thin mesh. Strange manoeuvrable sunglass lenses. A beak for a mouth, like a bird's. There were three thick leg appendages and many tentacle arms with three fingers. Then Lewis' candle light went out.

Despite having killed a Martian a short time ago, Reg only retained a crude notion of how the creatures actually looked. Now he was back in the darkness for his second killing. All he had taken from the previous incident was one thing. He knew he was stronger than the actual Martian. Once the vile creatures were outside their fighting machines, they were weak. Now Reg was the monster. He was the killing machine and the Martian was the feeble being at his mercy. The angry man revelled in the Martian's last desperate grasps of life. Reg gripped one of the tentacles. The creature had nowhere to run as it tried to pull away. It was choking from its wounds and gasping for breath.

The squeals were now weaker. Another blow of the scythe stopped the moaning altogether. Blow after blow sliced into the unseen being. Blood splashed with every angry chop. The only sound amid the hewing of chopped flesh was the cry of anger for each of Reg's swipes. In the blackness, he was drenched in more Martian blood. It was splattering all over him with each angry blow. The job was complete, but Reg continued to hack away. He was victorious and the foul alien was being mutilated in his fit of rage.

If there had been light, the Martian would be unrecognisable. Eventually, Lewis relit his candle. He had found it by the door of the storage room. Blanc was gently trying to persuade Reg to stop. He heard Lewis try to restrain the Frenchmen. He heard him say in a gentle voice. "Let him continue. Let him get it out of his system."

Blanc and Lewis stood outside the room. In the passageway. They waited patiently as Reg had exhausted himself. Finally, he stopped. He turned his gaze away from the bloodied pulp. The dimly lit sight of the pulverised meat was hacked beyond recognition. He was gasping for breath as he felt the rage slowly abate in his pulsating veins.

Reg began to regain his wits. Reason returned. He had killed two of the vile brutes now. His mother and nephew were safe. No one would ever hurt the ones he loved. They were safe, and the Martians could die.

"Reg, you all right, mate? Can we come in now?" asked Lewis respectfully standing his distance while the giant man's angry mood simmered down.

"I'm all right, Lewis," answered Reg. "That bloody thing is dead. I've done for the both of them Martians. They were having a go at my mum." He was like a stern little boy that had just proved a point.

Blanc looked on surprised and was disturbed by the violent horror. "Well, I am sure that no one else will upset your mother from this day on, my friend."

There was murmur of agreement from Lewis. "That is putting it mildly, Mr Blanc."

Lewis and Blanc slowly moved back into the room, the one remaining candle held aloft.

"Reg," said Quartermaster Blanc. "Put the blade down now, my friend. It is over. You have killed the beast."

Reg looked up at the wise old Frenchman, and nodded his head. Gently, he put the scythe down. "I want to get out of here now. I want some fresh air."

Lewis came forward and put a hand upon the giant man's shoulder.

"You were bloody marvellous, Reg. You showed them a thing or two today." He smiled at the big man, who did not look so inadequate now. "Breathe through your nose and let out air from the mouth. It calms you quicker."

Reg complied. He realised how shaken Blanc was. It was an unnerving calm after a traumatic and dreadful event. Now it was over. Yet all were more nervous than ever, pondering how they had come through the trials and dangers of the day.

Blanc scratched his side burns. "While things are happening, the actions we take motivate us. We have no time to think on the chances and risks we have taken. Now it is unsettling. But you did very well, Reg. Very well indeed."

Lewis nodded in agreement. "I know what you mean. Now that it is over, I can't stop shaking." He held up a hand that was trembling uncontrollably. "I need a good stiff drink." He looked at the faces of Reg and Quartermaster Blanc. "I think we all do."

"I'm not allowed to drink," said Reg childishly. "My mum only allows me one on special occasions. I've already had one earlier."

Lewis chuckled "She might make an exception for this once and grant another."

Reg smiled and allowed Lewis to lead him quietly out along the hallway. The French seafarer lingered

The Last Days of the Fighting Machine

for a moment, trying to decipher what the pulped and bloodied alien carcass might have looked like. After a moment, Blanc followed his British friends. They all squeezed through, with the little dog Gippy. They finally got to the foot of the winding stairs. All thankfully ascended. They were grateful once out before the daylight. Beautiful, clear blue sky that swamped the smouldering ruins about them. The smoke had thinned. The destruction was unimportant, they were alive and would remain so.

Mrs Steed came forward. She was anxious. Reg was covered in more alien blood. At least it was not his own.

"It's not Reg's blood, Mrs Steed," said Lewis quickly, trying to allay her fears. "It's the Martians. Reg killed it."

"My God, Reg," she remonstrated, but there was also pride and relief in her tone. She reached out and hugged the simple giant, grateful that her precious son had once again survived his ordeal. He wrapped his giant arms around her.

Jimmy came running forward. "Did you kill another one, Uncle? Did you get him with the scythe?"

Reg placed a hand upon the youngster's shoulder and pulled him towards them. They were all that remained of their family. They would fight to remain. "Nothing will beat us. Nothing ever," he muttered. He cuddled his mother and nephew tightly.

"These Martians are dying from all sorts of things," added Blanc. "Every day they are becoming more vulnerable because they are ill and getting weaker. From Scotland and Ireland there are land forces coming. They are landing and pushing forward. They will get closer to us with every passing day."

P.C. Llewellyn came forward and patted Reg on the shoulder. "I reckon a few weeks at most. Then we will start to see people."

"Do you think everything will be the way it was before?" asked Reg. "With the red weed gone as well?"

All looked about them, noticing the large green patches that were spreading in the fields. Upon the hedgerows, the red weed was pinking and fading away. Lewis nodded his head in agreement. "There seems to be more greenery every day. The red stuff is turning pink and going brittle. I don't think it can survive here. It was never meant to."

Blanc nodded. "Maybe these Martians were never meant to live here either."

"Be that as it may," added Llewellyn, becoming the local policeman again. "We will still need to go to ground before any of the land forces get here." He looked to Mrs Steed. "I think we should all return to the police station in Canewdon until then. Including you and your family, Mrs Steed. We will all be together and a little safer there. I have been living in the cells in the basement."

Reluctantly, Mrs Steed nodded her head in agreement. "I'll go. But at the first opportunity I'll be coming back here as soon as the soldiers come."

"Until the soldiers arrive then," Llewellyn smiled. "Let's go. I would like to leave this place as soon as possible."

All turned and began their journey towards Canewdon. Heading north-west across the fields but hugging the hedgerows as they left the smouldering ruins of Paglesham Churchend.

EPILOGUE

P.C. Adrian Llewellyn 13th September 1898

Today I went foraging towards Rochford with Quartermaster Blanc and Linville. We had been exploring derelict houses to see if there were any tinned foods. We were fortunate to find a few things. Upon coming out of one such property, we were shouted at and told to halt by armed soldiers. We raised our hands in fear and called back that we were foraging for tin foods, not trying to loot personal property. I went forward with my hands raised so that they might see my police uniform.

To our delight, four Scots soldiers emerged with their rifles raised. They wore Black Watch kilts. After satisfying them of our honourable intentions, they lowered their weapons, then came forward. They shook our hands warmly.

I could barely contain my delight and started asking them many questions. Mr Blanc did too. He introduced himself and Linville as sailors from F.S. *Ney*.

We were taken to their temporary headquarters and questioned by a Major Munro of The Black Watch Regiment. He released us with a small patrol of soldiers. He also gave us more food rations.

The delight on Mrs Steed's face was an absolute picture when we got back to Canewdon. Reg and Jimmy were whooping for joy. Lewis was trying to find out if any of the soldiers had alcohol. To his relief they did. We all ate and drank to the demise of the Martians. The invaders, we were told, had been dying in multitudes all over the country. The Queen had survived and had reached Balmoral. We were suddenly uplifted. More than we had been in a long time. We knew that there was something wrong with the Martians for a long time now. But to hear it first hand was glorious and truly gratifying for all.

P.C. Llewellyn.

God Save the Queen

Printed in Great Britain
by Amazon